A ROGUE TO ENSNARE

ROGUES OF THE LOWLANDS
BOOK FOUR

BY
HILDIE MCQUEEN

ARE YOU SIGNED UP FOR DRAGONBLADE'S BLOG?

You'll get the latest news and information on exclusive giveaways, exclusive excerpts, coming releases, sales, free books, cover reveals and more.

Check out our complete list of authors, too!

No spam, no junk. That's a promise!

Sign Up Here

www.dragonbladepublishing.com

Dearest Reader;

Thank you for your support of a small press. At Dragonblade Publishing, we strive to bring you the highest quality Historical Romance from some of the best authors in the business. Without your support, there is no 'us', so we sincerely hope you adore these stories and find some new favorite authors along the way.

Happy Reading!

CEO, Dragonblade Publishing

Additional Dragonblade books by Author Hildie McQueen

Rogues of the Lowlands Series
A Rogue to Reform (Book 1)
A Rogue to Forget (Book 2)
A Rogue to Cherish (Book 3)
A Rogue to Ensnare (Book 4)

Clan Ross Series
A Heartless Laird (Book 1)
A Hardened Warrior (Book 2)
A Hellish Highlander (Book 3)
A Flawed Scotsman (Book 4)
A Fearless Rebel (Book 5)
A Fierce Archer (Book 6)
A Haunted Scot (Novella)
Highland Knight (Novella)
Stones of Ard Cairn (Novella)

The Lyon's Den Series
The Lyon's Laird

Pirates of Britannia Series
The Sea Lord
The Sea Lyon

De Wolfe Pack: The Series
The Duke's Fiery Bride

PROLOGUE

April 1893
Glasgow, Scotland

"MILES," HIS MOTHER called out as he walked around the ballroom ensuring everything was in place.

He turned to find his beautiful mother, Her Grace Arabella Johnstone, waving him to come. The skirts of the emerald-green ballgown swished around her legs as she walked toward him.

"Mother, you have outdone yourself." He kissed her cheek, and she waved her hands impatiently.

"Everything has been done. All that we need is to be ready as the first carriages arrive. I wish for you to meet someone."

"Mother." He let out a long breath. "I warned you, no matchmaking."

His mother's right eyebrow lifted, a trait they shared when making a point. "Your father and I will have a grandchild before we die. Not just a grandchild, but an heir."

"I am an heir," Miles stated, lifting his arm to escort her to the front door. "You and Father could have had another son or two who would ensure someone to carry the title after me."

His mother shook her head, her green gaze pinning him. "This delusion of yours not to marry will end. If you do not choose a bride soon, your father and I will choose one for you."

Used to her repetitive comments about his marital status, Miles pushed back in annoyance. In truth, he had little desire to marry anytime soon, if at all.

"I have told you Mother, once I reach forty, if I am not married, you can arrange a marriage. I do not care to whom. It will be a formality so that I can procreate your much wanted heir."

"Why are you so unyielding?" His mother gave him an incredulous look. "Did we do something wrong that made you so hard-hearted against marriage?"

"I am convinced that the marriage vows do not mean much to most people. You and Father are a rare example for fidelity, of course."

He'd witnessed how unfaithful people could be. But his own friend Grant was a perfect example of the infidelity of women. Most of Grant's wealthy benefactors and lovers over the years had been married women. He himself had slept with women who were engaged or married to other men.

No. He would not marry anytime soon, only to find his wife in another man's bed.

Miles stood dutifully next to his parents to greet their guests. By the time the last ones arrived, he'd lost count of how many eager mothers had thrust their daughters in front of him, espousing the young women's incredible and sometimes unbelievable virtues. If not for standing next to his father, who slid him warning looks every time he started to grin, he would have burst out laughing several times.

"Come, Darling." His mother touched his arm. "I wish you to meet a delightful young woman."

Another one? "I've already met all the delightful young women in the room," Miles replied, not moving. "More than enough of them for the night."

Never deterred, his mother walked across the room, and he was forced to follow her just as the musicians began the first dance of the night.

She stopped in front of one of the overzealous mothers, next to whom stood a reasonably attractive younger woman. "Zinnia," his mother began. "I was just telling Miles he should dance with your beautiful Amelia."

Her attention returned to Miles. "Son, this is Amelia Blair."

The young woman, Amelia, stood so straight he wondered if she could bend. Her nose held up, she scanned him from head to toe, as if assessing whether or not he was worthy of a dance with her. It didn't matter to him one way or the other.

Miles bent at the waist. "Miss Amelia, would you do me the honor of this dance?"

Amelia held out a hand and he took it, placing it into the crook of his arm before leading her to the dance floor where they joined the other dancers. The young lady was a perfectly accomplished dancer, and just as boring and unappealing as the rest of the young ladies paraded before him. I do not think I'll bother dancing with her again, he thought. No use getting her, or her mother's, or even *his* mother's, hopes up. Nothing about Amelia Blair sparked his interest.

The entire time they danced, he kept an eye on the door for when Grant and his bride Wren entered. He'd instructed the attendants that they should be announced with much fanfare.

Thankfully just as the song ended, he noted Grant and his new bride entering. He extricated himself form Amelia. "The guests of honor have arrived."

Somehow she managed to hold her nose higher. "Oh yes. They are the reason for all of this. I had forgotten."

Her comment reinforced his decision that he would not dance with her again, nor ever seek her company. Not only was she uninteresting, another debutante made in the mold of all the others, but she was shallow and self-centered as well.

In contrast to the overly primped and spoiled young ladies of the ton, Grant's new wife Wren appeared radiant. Clearly awed by the décor of the ballroom, she was wide-eyed, smiling with obvious happiness, and absolutely resplendent. Dressed understatedly in a pale green ballgown and long-sleeved gloves, her only nod to flamboyance was an elegant hairstyle. Somehow, in spite of her simplicity, or maybe because of it, Wren was much prettier than most of the women in the room. She was of a humble social status, having worked as a servant since arriving in Glasgow. Miles knew it was her quiet beauty that had garnered Grant's attention and now, much to everyone's surprise, his heart as well.

As the newlyweds were announced, he returned to stand with his parents as they congratulated Grant and Wren and toasted to their happiness.

The gathering would go far into assuring Wren's acceptance into their circles. No one would dare snub her after the display of support by the Duke and Duchess of Spencer.

Once the announcement and introductions to several prominent couples were completed, Grant went to Miles, and they hugged. "Again, I thank you so much for this. This ball will make even the most haughty members of the Haute Ton accept Wren into their midst. I can't thank your parents enough for their mark of approval." Grant's eyes shone with gratitude.

Miles nodded. "Take her to meet them. I'll be honest with you—they are anxious to know what kind of woman could possibly tame a rogue like you, so they can arm themselves in finding a bride for me."

As he spoke, he noticed Amelia out of the corner of his eye. She was headed straight for him, but he pretended not to see her. Instead he leaned close to grasp Grant's shoulder. "I wish you nothing but the best, my friend. But I for one aim to remain a bachelor, and with that in mind, I need to leave before one particularly marriage-minded miss can make me dance with her again." He backed away then, Grant's chuckles following in his wake.

Hoping to take refuge behind a punchbowl, he rounded the table, keeping his eyes on his pursuer. Unfortunately, his attention elsewhere, he collided straight into a soft, feminine form.

Her squeal was followed by the sensation of cold liquid splashing on his arm. He looked down at his sleeve, and then over his shoulder. To his horror, the young woman with whom he'd collided with was obviously about to lose her balance. Unwilling to allow her to fall, especially as a result of his own inattention, Miles took a step toward her. Just as he caught her elbow, he slipped on the floor made slick by her cup of punch, spilled as she'd pinwheeled her arms in an attempt to remain upright. He tried to stop himself—and the young woman—from falling, but it was of no use. Together, they lost their fight with gravity.

"Oomph!" The woman let out a harsh breath as he landed atop her, and he lifted himself on his hands to rise off of her before more people saw them in a compromised position, in public, on the floor under a table. But then he caught sight of her face and stilled, utterly enchanted.

For beneath him was the most beautiful creature he'd ever seen. She had an oval face, a pert nose, and hair as dark as midnight and spilling in waves from her coif as pins scattered. Though he thought it possible he was made breathless because of their fall, still he was fairly certain it was her loveliness that made him forget how to breathe.

They lay, shocked face to shocked face. And then, she went limp as she looked up at him with pale blue, long-lashed eyes. Instead of falling into an embarrassed faint as would the rest of the young ladies he knew, this woman suddenly began shaking, with her pink lips split into a grin; to his shock, she began *laughing* while pushing him off of her and squirming out from underneath him in the most immodest of ways. "Oh dear. Mother will never let me hear the end of *this*."

He managed to spring to his feet so he could bend and help her up. As she rose, he realized that most of the punch had splashed onto her bodice and the floor. He only suffered a wet sleeve and had remained mostly dry.

"Siobhan, you are making a spectacle of yourself." Amelia had neared and stood with fists at her sides and with a furious curl to her upper lip. "Must you always make a mockery of our family with your actions?"

She gestured to the Duchess, making her way across the room to them, another woman—their mother, Zinnia, trailing behind.

"Your Grace, I beg you, excuse my sister's actions," Amelia said to his mother, then slid a glare at her sister, who gave her a bland look in return, something that made Miles find her even more attractive, though he could not possibly explain why.

Meanwhile, Amelia jabbed at Siobhan with one hand. "Apologize to Her Grace! And Lord Miles!"

"You've already met my sister," murmured the young woman in his ear. She took a sideways step to stand behind Miles and placed her hand on his upper arm while peeking over his shoulder. "I saw you dancing with her just a moment ago."

"Ah. Yes." Though he supposed society expected he should be dismayed by her clumsiness and lack of decorum, Miles found that he was pleased to play protector for the unusual—nay, unique—young lady, instead.

"It was I who ran into…Siobhan, I believe? I caused her to fall. This is not of her doing and there is nothing for which she must apologize," Miles clarified. "In fact, it is I who must apologize to you, Miss Blair, for my own clumsiness." He had to twist sideways to look at her. "How do you do?"

The pretty woman took a tentative step back and shrugged, then noting her mother nearby, straightened and gave him a soft smile. "I am well. It is nice to meet you, and rest assured, no harm has been done, my lord."

Amelia made a dismissive noise. "Come let us try to remedy your ruined dress, if that's even possible." She motioned for Siobhan to come out from behind him and follow her.

The young beauty slid a glance to him, her gaze moving from his eyes to his lips and then back to meet his eyes. She nodded her head in a quick bow and again, that smile danced on her mouth. "My lord, I look forward to the rest of this delightful evening." With that, she allowed Amelia to escort her away.

While his mother hurried to inspect him and ensure there

were no stains, and servants quickly cleaned the floor, his attention remained on the young woman—Siobhan, he reminded himself—being led away from the ballroom. Her mother had detached from his mother and had caught up to the daughters. She had grasped her younger daughter's upper arm and, with her face red and eyes blinking, appeared to be hissing like a steaming kettle in her ear. Obviously, she was giving the young miss a scathing tongue lashing.

"No," his mother warned as she noticed how he watched her leaving. "The younger Miss Blair is like an untamed cat. She is always causing one thing or another. According to rumors, her last antic happened when her carriage driver fainted. Reportedly, she climbed from the back of the carriage, and then jumped onto the horse's back to bring it to a stop. In the middle of Queen Street!"

"You do not say?" Miles fought not to smile. That would have been a sight he'd would have loved to have witnessed. "Did she really?"

His mother, realizing her story had only roused his interest, tried a new, potentially more scandalizing tact. "She rode the beast *astride!*"

Miles gave her a grin but refrained from telling her how much he wished he could have seen that for himself. Instead, he took his mother's arm and steered her away from the punch table. "If you must know, Mother, this incident is entirely my fault. I ran into her whilst trying to keep from the eldest Miss Blair," he replied. "Never fear. I'm not interested in pursuing her as a potential wife, fascinating a prospect as that may be." He reached to press his finger to her mouth as she opened it to protest. "Because, Mother, as you well know, I have no plan to pursue anyone."

She shut her mouth then, as expressions of disappointment and dismay warred on her face.

His father, Leon Archibald Johnstone, the Duke of Spencer, joined them. "Is everything well?"

"No." His mother's expression settled on determination, and he realized she had decided which course was best; she was going to discourage him from pursuing Miss Blair in spite of the fact that some kind of interest was better than none at all. "Your Grace, I just saw a gleam in his eye. And it was directed at the *worst* possible young woman."

Miles met his father's gaze, seeing curiosity and even a bit of indulgent humor there. He pointed to his own eyes. "Fear not, Father. No gleam." With that, he turned and walked away before his parents could produce another woman whom they considered more worthy of his interest.

Or worthier than the younger Miss Blair, he mused. He wondered if she'd left the ball, and where he might fall over her next. Perhaps, he mused, this night would turn out to be much more than another tiresome social gathering. And indeed it wasn't even an hour later when, across the room, furtive movement caught his attention. It was Siobhan, as she darted from behind curtains, past a large potted plant, and then slipped out, unchaperoned, into the garden.

He could not help but smile. She was a wild one, indeed.

CHAPTER ONE

May 1893
Glasgow, Scotland

WHEN THE CARRIAGE came to a stop in front of the Blair mansion, Miles let go of the breath he'd been holding. This was to be the first of many summer balls that he would be required to attend. If not for the fact his young sister, Penelope, was attending, he would not be there.

Penelope had recently turned sixteen, and in his opinion was not at all ready to be out in society. But there was no holding back the willful lass, who wished to attend as many balls as she could.

When he'd asked her about it, she'd giggled, stating that she wanted to see what all the fuss was about. He'd silently thanked God she showed little interest in courtship of any kind.

"My lord." The driver held open the door and he climbed down from the carriage. Once standing on solid ground, he ensured his soft gray overcoat was in order, sliding his hands down the front.

His parents' carriage, following behind, came to a stop once his pulled away, and he walked over to assist his mother and sister.

"You look very handsome." His mother's green gaze scanned over him. "I have always considered gray to be a good color for you. It brings out your eyes."

Penelope studied him for a moment. She wore a yellow

gown, which Miles was sure she'd picked out because of the brightness of the color. It was slightly garish for a debutante and not a popular shade, but his mother had not stopped her as the family was in no hurry for her to find a suitable husband.

In spite of the garish color, she was pretty, with an impish face, and upturned lips that made it seem as if she were always holding back laughter. Truth be told, she often was; she had a personality as bright as her dress. "Brother, you must introduce me to Siobhan Blair. She is the talk of the town for making you fall."

Miles gave his sister as bland a look as he could muster. "You were there. I am sure you met her that night."

"I did not," his sister insisted. "Corinne and I were occupied in the planetarium."

"Spying on couples?" He cocked an eyebrow but could not help laughing. "Minx."

Penelope giggled and took his arm. "Do not scold me. It is very enjoyable to be part of all of this."

"What about a husband? Have you considered that by being out in society, it is assumed you are prepared to marry?"

His heart danced happily when Penelope wrinkled her nose. "I do not want a husband. Mama agrees that I should wait at least another year."

"I also agree."

His father and mother were announced as they entered the ballroom, followed by him and then Penelope. They were ushered into a long ballroom. Windows had been placed at each end of the room, either looking over the long road in front of the house so people could see the arriving carriages, or peer into the gardens.

Despite not caring to be there, Miles had to admit the room was beautiful. Chandeliers hung every few feet, and under each was placed a round table with offerings of every appetizer imaginable or huge punchbowls filled with liquids of different colors.

Miles stood with his sister for a few moments before spotting Henry Campbell, who'd obviously been deserted by his lovely wife Hannah. He bid his sister to behave herself and went over to stand with his friend. As Miles neared, his friend gave a slight bow in acknowledgement. "I did not expect to see you here. If not for Mother's insistence, Hannah and I would have remained at home."

"Then we both have the same reason for being here."

With a good-natured grin, Henry nodded. "Mothers."

Henry's regard moved past him to where his family was. "Also in your role of protective brother then?"

"A bit. However, with Father present, I doubt any man without good intentions will go near Penelope. Fortunately, it turns out she has no desire to marry anytime soon. Her sole purpose for attending functions is to gather gossip with her partner-in-crime, Corrine McDaniel."

They accepted flutes of champagne from a passing server and made their way to the doorway near the windows that overlooked the gardens. The evening breeze filtered in, allowing for the room to remain a bit cool.

Strains of music began, and people made their way to the dance area at the front of the room. In no time, a lively country dance began in which he had no desire to join. But it seemed to remind his friend that he had a wife who might be otherwise inclined. "I best go in search of Hannah," Henry said, taking his leave to make his way across the room to find her.

Miles remained where he was. The combination of the breeze and music was perfect where he stood. From there he could easily move outside to evade anyone attempting to introduce him to what they deemed a suitable wife. There were none, of course, and never would be.

Across the room, he caught sight of Siobhan Blair, and his lips twitched as he caught himself readying to smile, lest anyone think he was actually enjoying himself, or considering engaging someone in a dance, himself. He watched as Siobhan danced with a young man whose name Miles could not recall but from the adoring glances the man gave Siobhan, was an ardent admirer.

Suddenly the young man's face crumpled with a pained expression. He lifted a foot and hopped in a circle. Siobhan took him by the elbow and helped him hobble to the sidelines. Now, Miles could not contain his grin at her contrite expression as she peered down at the man's foot. Then she appeared to make her goodbyes, leaving her lamed victim on the side of the dance floor. Miles' merriment increased when she turned away from her former partner and he noticed the way the corners of her lips turned up. The minx! She'd stomped the poor man's foot on purpose.

Then she began hurrying Miles' way—maybe to the door, to make her own escape?

The mischievous woman did not catch sight of Miles until she was upon him. Her eyes grew wide as she attempted to move past him to the balcony.

"Am I in the way of your hiding place?" Miles asked, studying the beauty. "By all means, pretend I am not here."

Her eyes narrowed. "I need fresh air. Nothing else."

"May I escort you then?" Miles held up his arm, knowing the woman had no choice but to accept it.

Upon her hand sliding into the crook of his arm, there was a stirring within him. Silent alarm bells rang in his head, and he took a deep breath, then slowly released it as they walked forward.

As soon as they reached the stone banister, Siobhan let go of his arm and peered over the side, looking toward the garden with a wistful expression, her body leaning forward. "Do you like large social events, Lord Miles?"

Her question was a simple one, but for whatever reason it felt like a test. Following her line of sight, he noted that the Blair gardens were very large, with plenty of places to hide and seek solitude or other pursuits it was best not to think about at the moment.

"I do not. I prefer gatherings of a more intimate nature. Dinner with the family, for instance. Or drinks with a few of my friends."

There was approval in her gaze. "Then you must understand what it is like for me, living here. Mother finds every excuse to host a party or ball. We host at least once a month." She let out a huff. "I go to the modiste so often, she no longer takes measurements."

"Is that why you have a reputation for causing mayhem?" he half-joked. Hers was a predicament indeed. If his family entertained that often, he would be put out as well.

She studied him. Like the time before when her icy-blue eyes had raked over him with interest. "You are a beautiful man. Why are you not married?"

Her bluntness caught him off guard, and he had to swallow to keep from choking on his drink. He recovered his composure and replied, "I am flattered you think so. I do not care for marriage." Perhaps he deserved her query; after all, he'd also been as blunt with his own question. She was sharp in more ways than one, he thought with admiration.

"Hmm." She shrugged. "Enjoy the festivities." With that, she hoisted up her skirts to expertly climb over the short banister and hopped down to the garden. Without a backward glance, she scurried into the garden and disappeared.

It was as if she'd never been there. A most interesting creature, Siobhan was. A chuckle erupted from him as he considered her antics and the reasons for them.

"Lord Miles!" Amelia Blair, the older sister appeared. "I wondered where you'd gone." She scanned the gardens. "Have you seen my sister?"

"I did, earlier." His reply was not a lie, but neither was it the full truth.

Her pert nose in the air, she looked at him as if expecting him to carry the conversation. "You look lovely tonight, Miss Blair." Miles attempted a polite expression, but probably failed. As they did for the minx who'd run into the garden, these balls, and the need to converse and be social made it feel like a prize fighter had a chokehold on his neck.

"Will you be joining the festivities or spending your time out here?" Amelia studied him with obvious admiration, judging by the way her eyes raked over his face and down to his chest, making him feel like a choice lamb chop. "Mother insisted I find you and allow you to sign my dance card."

"Of course. It will be my honor to do so." Though that was a lie, he had no choice. Social niceties required he be polite to his hostess whether it was sincere or not. Miles took the proffered card and pencil and scribbled in his initials.

When he returned the card, Amelia's lips curved. It was only then that he saw the resemblance between her and Siobhan. Although Amelia was attractive, she was of a paler complexion, with golden highlights in her brown hair. Unlike her sister's ice-blue eyes, Amelia's were hazel. But the main difference between the sisters was the way Amelia held herself in very high regard, and it was obvious that she expected attention. It was also obvious that this sister loved the festivities her mother hosted by the way she constantly looked about the room with an excited expression on her face.

Meanwhile, Siobhan didn't seem to realize—or care—how beautiful she was and instead, fled from a situation where she'd garner attention.

"Do you enjoy large social events, Miss Blair?" Miles asked the woman the same question Siobhan had asked him a few moments earlier.

Amelia leaned toward him, hand over her bosom. "I adore them. The opportunity to dress beautifully and enjoy people's company and music is so exciting, is it not?" She didn't wait for Miles to reply. "I cannot think of anything I enjoy more."

Just then something seemed to catch the woman's attention in the ballroom. Yet, she seemed reluctant to leave his side, so he made it easier. "I must see about my sister. May I escort you back inside?" He offered her his arm and led her back into the crowd.

Once there, he had no choice but to put his name on the dance cards of other young women, but only enough to satisfy his mother that he was indeed searching for a suitable wife. As soon as he could, he escaped outside to walk through the peaceful and quiet garden. He didn't expect to run into anyone as the weather was cool enough that the ballroom remained comfortable.

He'd yet to see Siobhan again and he wondered if she'd snuck to her bedchamber for the evening.

The sound of whispers got his attention. Whoever the two were sounded like women. He neared a bush and peered past it to see a couple oblivious to how easy they were to spy. In a tight embrace, they kissed with wild abandon. But the giggle and whispers came from a tall wall of nearby bushes, and he leaned into it, to find two young women hidden among the branches and watching the lovers as they embraced. One of them wore a familiar, bright yellow dress.

"Penelope?" He reached in and yanked his sister by the arm. "What are you doing?"

His sister's wide eyes moved from him to the couple, still unaware of their observers. They'd pulled apart and were now walking farther into the garden. Miles shuddered to think what his sister and accomplice would have witnessed if they'd followed the obviously enraptured couple.

He turned to address his sister's accomplice. "Corrine, come out at once." Miles cringed at his fatherly tone. "What are you doing? Look at you two. Your hair is askew, and gowns crumpled."

Penelope reached up to push a dangling yellow bow from her hair and back into her dark curls. It flopped over her forehead, seeming to have given up any desire to function. Meanwhile, Corrine ran her hands frantically down her grass-stained skirts. "Mother will be most put out."

"Well, it is clear that neither of you can return inside in this state," Miles said, looking from one to the other.

His sister crossed her arms over her body; a second bow fell out of her hair to the ground. "I did not expect for these gowns and hairstyles to be so easy to ruin."

Corrine joined her friend in a show of solidarity by crossing her arms as well. "I stumbled into the bush and Penelope tried to help me, only to fall in as well."

"That is quite a dangerous bush it seems," Miles replied in a flat tone. "Spying on the couple who was kissing had nothing to do with you remaining there?"

His sister frowned and tossed her head. "Brother, you should stop chastising us and help us return inside. We must find a powder room and repair what we can."

"I will help you." Siobhan suddenly appeared at his elbow. She'd materialized from somewhere in the garden. "We can take the back stairs to my bedchamber." She motioned for the girls to follow as she turned to lead the way.

Miles caught up with the beauty and fell into step beside her. "You seem flushed, Miss Blair. Did you leave company to join us?"

She slid a glance up at him from the corners of her eyes. "If you must know, I was stargazing when an adventurous couple happened to decide the perfect place to…enjoy each other's company was directly in my line of sight." She blew out a breath. "I had to slip away before they noticed me. Or before I saw too much."

Miles pressed his lips together to keep from laughing. "So you enjoy the stars, but not love?"

It was comical to see her look over her shoulder as if expecting the couple to appear. "What they were doing was not love." She lowered her voice to a whisper and leaned closer. The scent of citrus blooms surrounded him. "It was *lusting*, my lord."

Penelope hurried to catch up with them; apparently spying on trysts wasn't the only thing she enjoyed. "What is 'lusting'?"

He opened his mouth to tell her to never mind, but Siobhan saved him from having to play the protector of their virtue. It made him wonder how much of the acts of love—and lust—this particular young minx understood, herself. She might have been young, but was it possible she wasn't inexperienced?

"Come. Hurry girls, lest we be spotted." Siobhan took both girls by the hands, and he let them go as they hurried away toward the side of the house, disappearing from his sight into the darkness.

He returned to the ballroom, and as soon as he went in, his mother moved quickly toward him. "Have you seen your sister?" Her eyes were wide with worry. "She and Corrine seem to be missing."

Miles nodded. "No worries, Mother. I found them in the garden. They were in a bush spying, on a couple who was kissing."

"Oh my." His mother covered her mouth with her hand.

He continued, "Siobhan Blair took the pair up to her bed-chamber to repair their appearances."

"Goodness," his mother said, looking toward the interior of the room. He spotted Corrine's mother making a beeline for them.

Blast. Miles took his mother's arm and led her toward the woman. "The fact of the matter is, neither of them are ready to be out yet. I think this should be Penelope's last ball for the season."

"I agree. Hopefully your father will not notice her absence tonight." She left his side to approach Corrine's mother.

He left the women so they could discuss what had occurred and strolled to the door. He'd had enough of this event.

"Lord Miles, I do believe it is time for our dance." Amelia blocked his exit.

He stopped a rude epithet from leaving his lips just in time. Instead, he screwed on a smile. He would make quick work of this and then depart. "Of course," Miles replied, offering his arm.

Just before the dance ended, Siobhan and the two younger women made their reappearance. Penelope looked no worse for the wear, her hair perfectly coiffed. Corrine's dress was pressed, and only because he'd been aware of its earlier state did he notice the grass stains.

Both his mother and Corrine's hurried to them, his mother speaking to Siobhan, who smiled at whatever was said.

The four went toward the punch bowl and served themselves while talking. It was obvious to Miles that his mother pretended all was well, keeping up the charade of chatting and enjoying the evening. Corrine's mother was not as adept at acting as his mother. Instead of pretending pleasantries, the woman stared daggers at her daughter.

Siobhan remained with them, as if ensuring the girls remained out of trouble. It was an interesting and startling idea, considering that he'd been warned of her unsuitability and wild, unladylike behavior.

The music stopped. He came out of his revelry and turned his focus back to Amelia. He bowed. "Thank you for this dance."

"You are most welcome, my lord." She curtseyed gracefully, but as usual, didn't spark any attraction in his heart.

Instead, he hurriedly returned Amelia to where her mother was, then turned and left before the women could engage him in additional conversation. Instead, he quickly went to where his mother—and Siobhan—were.

"Thank you for your help, earlier," Miles said, meeting her gaze.

"There is no need to thank me. I found myself in similar situations many a time." Her eyes twinkled when she met his eyes with her own.

Miles could not keep from smiling. "That does not surprise me." He held out his arm. "A dance, Miss Blair?"

For a moment he thought she'd decline, but to his surprise, she slipped her hand onto the crook of his elbow. While guiding her to the dance floor, looks of surprise and curiosity followed them, especially from his mother.

But the regard of others didn't matter. He kept his focus on

Siobhan and on her serene expression. It was as if she'd donned a mask. One for polite society, held perfectly in place while being noticed by others. The breathlessly laughing miss who'd knocked him to the floor was gone, as was the spirited young woman who'd vanished over the railing into the garden earlier that evening, or the competent rescuer of innocents he'd encountered later. He wasn't sure he liked this subdued, society appropriate version of her. Instead, he preferred the spirited and fascinating Siobhan. The one his parents found "unsuitable".

The music began. It was a waltz, and he placed his hand on the small of her back, leading her in the fast-paced dance, their feet barely touching the floor as they moved in a large circle with the other couples. She was an excellent dancer, with no signs of the clumsy woman who'd stomped on her partner earlier in the evening. Although they kept a respectable distance, the feel of her hand in his felt intimate.

He flexed his fingers just enough for her to feel his other hand upon the slight curve of her back. Her eyes met his, and she lifted her right brow in response to his flexing fingers. It was not in question, but more of an "I am aware of what you are doing," look.

Around and around they moved, almost as if floating on air, so in tune were they to one another. Miles leaned to speak into her ear. "Why did everyone look so shocked to see you dancing?"

"I pretend not to be able to dance and rarely am asked more than once by the same gentleman."

He laughed, earning him curious looks from those nearest. "And yet, it is obvious to me that you are an accomplished dancer. But our encounter in the garden at the start of the evening—after you trod on that man's foot, may I add—proves you are, in fact, a woman of many talents, Miss Blair. At least talents of evasion and, perhaps, even mystery."

"If you only knew, my lord," she quipped, her voice dryly amused.

The song slowed and then, the piece came to an end. It had not lasted nearly long enough in Miles' opinion. He wanted more time with her. As the musicians lowered their instruments and the crowd began to chatter, their gazes locked and it was as if for the first time in his life, Miles understood what it was like to come face to face with the one person who understood you at only a glance. The startling acknowledgment shook Miles.

Siobhan placed her hand in the crook of his arm, and he covered her hand with his as he led her from the dance floor. He surprised himself as he blurted, "May I call on you, Miss Blair?" He'd never expected to call on any woman. After all, he was devoted to his bachelorhood. But still—he craved to know the intricacies of this enigmatic woman even more than he wanted to avoid entanglement of any kind.

Her brow crinkled. "It is best you do not. I cannot imagine the fits my sister will have if you call on me instead of her, as she has set her mind to having you as a suitor."

Miles gave a slight nod. Perhaps it was for the good, since he didn't want to encourage rumors or worse, encourage his mother to press harder upon finding him a wife of her own liking. He shrugged, hoping he didn't sound too blase. "Very well. I'd hoped to hear more about your plans for the summer, but I understand your reasoning."

For a long moment, she studied him, and he hated how much her perusal affected him. What did she see as she gazed at him? And why did he care? He needed to get away from this woman, as much as he wanted to spend as much time as he could with her.

He let go of her hand and stepped back, so their contact was broken. But just as he was about to turn away, she opened her mouth to speak and he paused, unable to leave her until he knew what she was going to say. "I will be at the market square tomorrow, in front of Saint Sebastian's, late morning." With that, she turned and hurried away from him.

As he walked back toward his mother and sister, he peered over his shoulder in the direction Siobhan had gone. She'd disappeared from the ballroom, but he had a feeling she wouldn't move as easily from his thoughts.

CHAPTER TWO

IT WAS EARLY the next day when Siobhan entered the dining room. Her father sat at one end of the table, with a simple breakfast of toasted bread and an egg. He was reading the newspaper, but glanced up at her as she arrived in the room.

"As I expected, it is only us this morning, Lamb." His warm gaze met hers. "Your mother came to bed quite late. I imagine Amelia did as well."

Siobhan neared and kissed his cheek. "Good morning, Father. I went to bed very early."

"You should make more of an effort to be social," he chided gently.

"I am more like you than Mother. I prefer quiet gatherings of only a few people to large balls and so much activity. It makes my head swim."

Although her father nodded in understanding, he continued to speak against her lack of social involvement. "Your mother and I wish for you and Amelia to find suitable husbands. You managed to miss last year's social scene. This year, we expect more of an effort."

"Very well, Father," Siobhan said, sitting near him after getting herself a scone, some jam, and a couple of pieces of crispy bacon. She poured tea and peered at the doorway. "I suppose the staff is sleeping in as well."

Another annoying result of so many gatherings was the fact that their staff was often too tired to see to them the following day. Cook and a pair of her helpers ensured they were fed, but the rest of the staff was given the day off. This, of course, was unfair to Cook, so therefore they were given several days off the following week or whenever it was convenient for the family.

"So have you, then?" Her father chewed his food and peered at her over his spectacles. Owen Blair was a tall, slender man with gentle blue eyes and dark hair that begged to be cut or even combed, for that matter. Although he'd inherited well and managed the Blair fortune for his sister and brother, it was evident he would have preferred the life of a historian, as he spent most of his days in his dusty study poring over historical books and attending such lectures.

Siobhan swallowed and sipped from the teacup. "Have I what, Father?"

"Found someone suitable?"

It was shocking when her mind went directly to Lord Miles. That the man entered her thoughts was natural, she considered, as he was the only person outside of her household with whom she'd had an actual conversation with in the last several days.

From what she'd observed, like her, he was not at all ready to marry. Quite the contrary, he seemed to find ways to hide from overly ardent pursuers and mothers eager to shove their daughters in front of him. Despite the lack of interest in marriage, however, he *did* pique her curiosity. Especially because he'd asked to call on her.

What exactly was Miles looking for?

The tall, well-built man was quite handsome, Siobhan had to admit, his hazel eyes a stunning contrast to his caramel skin. With stark slashes for brows, a chiseled jaw and sumptuous lips, his looks caused many a young woman to vie for his attention.

"Siobhan?" his father prompted.

"Oh... yes. I danced with Michael MacDonald. He seems... er..." She paused, considering, before coming up with a suitable description. "Adequate." She shrugged. "I may see him again at the next ball or whatever event Mother has planned for us."

"A musicale." Her mother walked into the room, her complexion pale and purpled under her eyes. "I had to come down and see about…" She waved her hand, not finishing the sentence.

"The social papers have not been delivered yet, my dear," her father said. "It is much too early for there to be any word of last night's event."

Her mother didn't seem convinced. "Rose!" she called out. "Rose!"

Siobhan chuckled. "You gave everyone the day off. I believe no one is up and about as yet, Mother."

At the reminder, her mother motioned to Siobhan. "Be a dear and pour tea for your mother. I am quite parched."

As she rose to pour the tea, she said, "I am going with Henriette to the mission today. I can stop at the printing press." Siobhan spoke quickly in a carefully casual tone. Saturday mornings were her favorite time of the week. With her best and dearest friend, it was the day she went to help at the shelter for the poor and also visited with a widowed, sickly young woman, Susan, who had three young children. Of course, Mother did not approve of the activity, though one would assume having a daughter with a charitable heart was better than one who could dance and flirt and be more of an ornament than a caring human being.

She wasn't surprised when Mother said, "Honestly Siobhan, you can catch something there. Why do you insist on going instead of sending one of the staff to do…whatever you do there?" Her mother looked at the doorway as if expecting the elusive Rose to appear. "Where is that girl?"

Her husband peered at his wife and smiled. "You should return to bed and rest, dear. There is no need to fret over the social pages. They will not be out for delivery until this afternoon."

WHEN THE CARRIAGE came to a stop in front of her friend Henriette Perot's house, her friend appeared and hurried to join her. Once seated next to Siobhan, she let out a breath. "That was quite close. Mother overheard my conversation with Jean-Pierre and called out to ask what we were up to."

Jean-Pierre was Henriette's older brother, who joined them on these excursions to ensure they were safe. Often he'd remain until they exited Susan's home and then he'd ride away. As on most days, the man's horse came into view and as he mounted, he peered toward the carriage.

"He pines for Amelia. He's always hopeful she will join us," Henrietta explained in her thick French accent. *"Mon pauvre frère. He should give up."*

Although both of Henriette's parents were born in France, her mother, Eva, was of Scottish descent. The Perots had moved to Scotland after Eva Perot had inherited a valuable mansion and a sizeable bank account as she was the only heir of a grandfather she'd never met.

From the first time they'd met during pianoforte lessons, Siobhan and Henrietta had become best friends, mostly due to the fact that neither had musical talent and their ever-suffering tutor would walk in circles murmuring to herself how much she missed teaching at a musical arts school with students who could actually play.

Henriette was petite, with bright eyes and curly reddish hair, like her mother's. The mixture of a French and Scottish accent was delightful to Siobhan, who was one of the few who could understand her when she became overly excited and spoke in a mixture of both languages.

"Cook gave me what we need to make chicken stew today," Siobhan exclaimed, holding up her filled basket.

"That will be good. I instructed the driver to take us to the nearby market. From there we can bring some food to the mission and buy whatever else Susan and her *enfants* might use. I also brought some liniment and tincture for her," Henriette announced.

"That's perfect." Siobhan smiled.

As the driver drove to the market by the church, she peered out the window to note that already many people were out and about. Granted, most of them were people of little means who were forced to work every day to provide for their families.

Thoughts of families, children, wives and husbands brought her mother's most recent husband-hunt to mind. "I saw the handsome Lord Miles last night," Siobhan told her friend. "He asked to call on me."

Henriette's eyes rounded and she spoke reverently. "*Ooh la, ma cherie.* You must tell me everything. What did he say? What did *you* say?"

Despite the fact that just thinking of the arrogant but beautiful man brought butterflies to her stomach, Siobhan was sure nothing would ever come of their acquaintance. "First, we spoke just outside the ballroom. I was headed to the gardens, to..." She didn't finish the sentence. Instead, she shrugged.

"To escape," Henriette finished for her, with a grin.

Siobhan nodded, grateful to have a friend who understood her so well. "He stopped me and asked where I was going. We spoke of inconsequential things, and then I continued to the garden. Moments later, he was out there, chastising his sister and her friend."

Henriette leaned in to ensure she did not miss a word. "I cannot imagine what he must look like, dressed like a prince and standing in the moonlight."

"He looked the same." Siobhan waved away any comments that her friend planned to continue with. "I had to take his sister to my bedchamber and repair her hairstyle. Apparently, she'd tangled with a bush. After that, he asked me to dance a waltz with him, and then, he asked to see me again."

"What was your response?" Henriette asked, leaning even closer.

"Goodness Henriette, why do you not just sit on my lap?"

Siobhan said, laughing. "I told him Amelia had her sights on him and that I would be here this morning." She motioned to the church and the market stalls which were set up next to it.

Her friend whipped her head around to look outside. "Do you think he will come?

"Of course not," Siobhan replied. "This is not the part of town people like him frequent. I doubt he knows where Saint Sebastian's is."

"But what if he does?"

Siobhan shook her head. "He will not."

WITH OVER-LADENED BASKETS, Siobhan and Henrietta hurried to the shelter. Not only did they carry food, but the driver followed with the bandages, tonics, and other items they'd procured at the market stalls.

A sturdy woman with gray-streaked hair pulled into a tight bun met them at the entrance to the shelter and took the supplies from them. It was not a safe place; some of the people who sought shelter there suffered from different afflictions, some contagious, so they rarely went inside.

"It is much too dangerous in there for you," the woman repeated what she said most Saturdays. "Several people are sick with consumptive issues." Then she inhaled deeply. "I come out here every so often to catch a breath of fresh air."

"Are there any young ones?" Siobhan asked. "I have some dolls in the carriage."

"Not today, thankfully," the woman replied. "Just yesterday, a woman with a small girl left. The woman's father came to fetch her."

"That is good," Henriette stated. "That they find family."

From there, they decided to walk to Susan's house and the driver went back to the carriage. He would wait outside on the street until they emerged. Siobhan knew that he often took advantage of this time to visit with his people. They lived just a few streets away.

Just before entering the building where the widow lived, Siobhan scanned the street. She looked over her shoulder, noting that only Jean-Pierre was there. He spoke to the driver and then rode away. After that, there was no one else she knew on the street.

"What is it?" Henriette asked.

Siobhan shook her head. "Nothing. We should hurry. The young ones will be anxious to see what we bring."

Susan lived in a place consisting of three combined rooms. One was used as a kitchen and dining room, the other two were bedrooms. In one the two older children slept, the other Susan shared with her youngest.

After they knocked, the door opened, and a dirty little face peered up at them. Upon recognizing them, the girl, Emily, moved back, her mouth curving into a smile showcasing several missing teeth. Her brother, Billy, two years younger at six joined the girl, his eyes wide with excitement.

Like every Saturday before, the first task was to go to the window and call out to the driver for water from the nearby well. They lowered a bucket on a rope, which was filled and hoisted up several times to fill a tea kettle, and a stew pot. They set the vessels on the small stove to heat. Once the water boiled, they filled a small tub, adding some of the cold water so it wasn't too hot, and they began the task of bathing the children. Emily and the baby, Sarah, were bathed together, then Billy took a hurried bath that she was sure he enjoyed even though he complained about it. As he was dried and dressed in clean clothes, more bath water was heated so that it could be added as needed, and so that once the children were clean, they could help Susan to bathe.

Although the woman was weak she did her best to ensure the children were fed and cared for.

"Everything is very clean," Siobhan told the young mother. "You should not do so much."

"My neighbor comes and helps with cleaning and cooking. In exchange, I share what you bring me on Saturdays."

"Bravo," Henriette said. "It is good that you can do that. You do need the help."

While Susan bathed, Siobhan set the cut-up chicken to boil along with chopped carrots and potatoes. She'd had to persuade Cook to teach her to make simple meals, though once she knew why Siobhan wanted to learn, she often prepared the ingredients ahead of time. She'd have to tell Cook that the widow shared what they brought each week. She knew she'd be willing to prepare even more food to give to the little family. Charity wasn't something she found shameful, and she appreciated that Siobhan was willing to give what she could to those less fortunate.

As Siobhan worked on the meal, the oldest children stood at the doorway and watched with rapt attention. She knew it wasn't just for the good stew that they waited, but she enjoyed stretching out their anticipation. When it seemed like they were about to explode with anticipation, she brought out the bag of sweets she'd purchased at the market just as she did every week. Predictably, they squealed with delight and her heart warmed at how such a simple thing could bring the little unfortunates such enjoyment. She held up the bag. "You may choose one each. I will give you one more after you eat, and then I'll give the bag to your Mama to save for the week."

The sweets disappeared into their greedy mouths, and then they returned to the bedroom where Emily and Sarah played with rag dolls Henriette had made for them and Billy lined the toy horse Siobhan had bought him this week up with the others she'd given him in the "stable" he'd created under the bed.

"How do you feel?" Siobhan asked the much-too-thin mother. "Have you been eating?"

"I eat thick porridge every day," Susan assured. "Beans and bread as well. But I can only eat it a little bit at a time, or I get sick."

"A doctor should see you," Siobhan stated. "Perhaps your neighbor will look after the bairns, and I can take you to the clinic."

"I am feeling much better. There is no need," Susan replied. Still, although she tried to sound strong, her voice was barely above a whisper.

They remained for a while longer. Once the children were seated and eating, Siobhan and Henriette went about sweeping the bedrooms and ensuring the beds were bug free. After, they placed the leftover food into a smaller pot, washed the dishes, and poured out the bath water. Henriette sat down and braided the girl's hair, while Siobhan rubbed liniment into the sick woman's back and shoulders. As she did so, she observed the woman's bony frame, her protruding ribs, and even the bumps in her spine. There was no denying that Susan was incapable of providing for her small family but without family for her to rely on, there wasn't much they could do and no place for the children except for the workhouse, a place none of them wanted to consider. "Are you sure there is no one who can help you? Take you in?" Siobhan asked. It was not the first time she'd asked, promising to find a parent, sibling or even her dead husband's family. But each time Susan insisted there was no one who could or would help.

They'd left her in a chair to watch over her children as they played on the now-clean floor. The woman seemed to be getting weaker by the week. There had to be something they could do.

"We must get you to see a doctor. When was the last time you were treated?" Siobhan asked.

The woman's lips curved into a soft smile. "Not since the last time you brought me, Miss."

"I will see about it then." Satisfied that all that could be done was, Siobhan called the oldest child over. "Emily, this food is meant to last as long as possible, so do not gobble it up." She pointed to the bread and cheese, instructing her how to portion it for the week. She then helped her to portion it out and talked to her until she was sure the girl understood what she needed to do to keep them all fed if not completely full.

Then she spoke to Susan. "We are leaving enough items for some mutton stew and porridge. Have the woman that helps cook it over the next few days."

"I will. God bless you, I do not know how I could do without you." The sick woman's eyes were shiny with tears. "You are angels."

Perhaps, Siobhan thought, but she wished she had the power of an angel to do more for the struggling family. After placing a couple coins on the tabletop for coal and whatever else they'd need, both she and Henriette left.

Just before exiting onto the street, Siobhan spotted a familiar-looking lord through the glass panels in the door, sitting on his horse by the carriage.

She froze. Obviously, not expecting her sudden stop, Henriette bumped into her. But that didn't matter. What did was—*was it really him?*

It wasn't possible. Was it? Why was he here, really?

"What is it?" Henriette asked, leaning to peer over her shoulder, and follow her line of sight. "Oh! *C'est lui.* Lord Miles!"

Although he was there, a part of her brain didn't comprehend the sight of him. He was so very out of place as he guided his fine riding horse closer to the carriage and spoke to the driver. While speaking, he looked in their direction, seeming to see them through the dirty glass.

"What in the world is he doing here?" Siobhan asked in a whisper.

"I believe you mentioned on the way here that you'd told him where you'd be this morning," Henriette replied with a laugh in her voice. "He came."

"Well then…he is late, and I told him I'd be at the shelter and the market." Siobhan turned away from the window. "The shelter worker must have told him we'd be here. If he tells anyone about us being here, our mothers will forbid us from ever returning."

"You must speak to him," Henriette told her with a pinched expression. "Beg him not to speak a word of it."

It was bad enough that Henriette's brother knew what they

did and agreed to look the other way, but it was a totally different matter that Miles Johnstone would now know. She was sure he'd not approve and—like her mother—would ask questions about why they didn't send servants to do their charity work.

They thought about waiting until he rode away, but it didn't appear that he was leaving anytime soon. In fact, he'd dismounted and stood beside his horse with the reins in his fist. He wasn't going anywhere. As much as it broke her heart, they had no choice but to leave the building and confront him.

They made their way to the carriage. Prepared for what was sure to be an exhausting exchange, she motioned to the driver. "I will be a few moments. Pick me up at the tea shop around the corner."

With purposeful steps, she walked to where Miles stood managing to be a picture of calm gentility even in the dirty, busy street. Despite the anxiety gnawing at her stomach, Siobhan could not stop herself from admiring him. Tall, well-built, and finely dressed in dark brown and riding boots, he was so utterly handsome.

She lifted her chin, attempting to appear dismissive and not seem to be overwhelmed by his attractive appearance. "My lord, I did not expect to see you."

He touched the brim of his riding hat, while his eyes locked with hers. "Miss Blair. I didn't expect that you would be inside such a place." He looked from her to the building across the cobblestoned street. "A tenement, of sorts?"

As he squinted toward the building, Henriette hurriedly climbed into the carriage, peering at them through the window.

"So it would seem." She began strolling, and he walked beside her, leading his horse along behind him on the side of the road. If he considered it strange that she did not have a chaperone, he didn't say anything. In truth, Scotland was much less stringent about such things compared to society in England. It was something for which Siobhan was eternally grateful.

"My friend Henriette and I purchase food and other necessary items and bring them to the shelter. We also bring whatever we manage to collect throughout the week. There is much need, my lord." She deliberately left out the part about visiting Susan, hoping to steer the conversation away from the subject.

"Indeed. Except the shelter isn't in that building, obviously. Which leads one to wonder, why do you then go into such an unsafe place after? Your driver tells me you do so every week." His voice was smooth, genteel, and somehow very stern. Of course. He barely knew her, yet he'd apparently decided her welfare and whereabouts were somehow his business.

Annoyance at the fact she had to explain herself boiled inside her. Of course he would never understand. Noblemen like Miles Johnstone had others do such work for them. He would never lower himself to see after people like Susan and her children.

Drat. Worse, he wasn't about to leave it alone. Her excuse hadn't worked, obviously. She'd have to remember to tell the driver to not be so open with people about what she did. Not that it mattered, now. With a sinking heart, she decided to be honest with him, since it appeared she had no other choice. "We visit a young widow, Susan, who is very sickly and has a hard time caring for her children, Emily, Billy, and baby Sarah. Henrietta and I got to know her through our volunteer work. When she'd stopped coming to the mission suddenly, we had to find out what happened."

"So you deliver to her?"

Not knowing Miles well, Siobhan had no way of extricating what he thought or felt by his expression. The man seemed to wear a mask—albeit a handsome one—that didn't allow for any expression of emotion. She supposed she understood. After all, didn't she often don a similar mask herself?

There was so much that society expected, but so little that they actually knew. She sighed.

"Henriette and I deliver food and do some things to help. We bathe the children, bring them things they need or can use, and cook a meal. It is not much, but I feel better knowing that for a few days out of the week, they eat well and are clean." She paused before adding, "It seems the least we can do. Honestly, we should do more but are stopped because 'proper' young ladies do not go inside—as you put it—'such a place'." *There*. Take that, she thought. With any luck, he'd feel some compassion, something that few in their society seemed to possess.

His brows lowered and he gave her a quizzical look, almost as if he had many more questions, but had lost the ability to formulate them. "I see."

At his words, she decided it was best to charge forward with her request. Siobhan placed her hand on his forearm to stop him from taking another step. When he turned to face her, his regard so intent, she inhaled sharply.

"I must ask…no. I must beg of you. *Please* do not say anything about… about this to anyone. My mother will forbid me from returning and it is important I ensure the family is taken care of. Without our help, Susan could die, and her children will end up in the workhouse. Henriette and I pay for her rent out of our pin money, but there is so much more needed."

"She has no family?" he asked. That he hadn't responded to her request was worrisome.

"There is none. I believe her parents have perished and her dead husband was an orphan. They are very poor." She pressed his arm with her fingers, feeling the warmth of it through the fabric of his riding jacket. "Will you keep my secret?" Siobhan asked again, noting they'd arrived at the tea shop. She met his eyes with her own. "Please."

Miles nodded. "For the moment. However, I must say what you already know. This is a dangerous area. It is not safe for women such as yourself and your friend to be about without someone looking out for you. It is not enough to leave your driver outside, because once you are inside that building, what if harm comes to you?"

Sending a silent prayer to heaven, Siobhan was glad Henriette's brother had left early that day. Otherwise, she was sure Miles would have much to say to him about covering up what they did.

"My lord," she began, needing to ensure that he understood why they did what they did. "The people of our social circle have galas where there is an overabundance of food and drink. Money is given for causes, but no one ever ensures to see if indeed the money is spent for the causes, or if it is recycled for another gala." Siobhan hoped the absurdity, the avarice, and the worthlessness of it all occurred to him now, if it hadn't ever before.

She took a breath and continued, "Do you know that even though there have been galas and collections for the shelter, it has never received any of that money? Instead, every so often a wagon will come and deliver a few used blankets or perhaps, already-worn shoes and cast off clothes. It is rarely enough to make a difference."

He studied her for a moment, his expression grave and thoughtful. "I must admit. That is very surprising."

Reassured by his words, she continued, "What we throw away after a social gathering could feed every person living in that building twice over. I know what I do makes little difference to the whole of impoverished people, but the few coins I spend to purchase items that I deliver to them makes a huge impact to Susan and her bairns. The help Henriette and I give that small family means the world to them. It keeps them alive. So I do not care what society deems 'proper' or 'appropriate' for a young lady. The fact of the matter is, my lord, I will not stop."

CHAPTER THREE

M ILES HAD TO admit, Siobhan Blair was like no other woman he'd ever met. Not only was everything she did unconventional, but she was unrepentant. It seemed whatever she set her mind to, she did, and with zeal.

Standing in front of the tea shop, with the reins of his horse clutched in his fist, the aroma of fragrant tea mixtures and pastries whirled around them as she pleaded her case, explaining why she'd taken on the yoke of humanitarian. From the enthusiasm in her voice and sparkle of her eyes, it was obvious this was something she was passionate about, and truly, as she pled her case, he could not blame her for it. There was nothing to be had but admiration.

Was she as passionate in every area of her life? It was an intriguing thought, and as she made her appeal, Miles considered her graceful gestures and womanly curves, unable to stop his mind as it wandered to dangerous territory, especially when standing outdoors in front of the vibrant woman.

He realized she had stilled and was waiting for his response. He reined in his desire and set his mind back on course. "I must admit to finding your enterprise to be most unexpected for a woman of our social status. But you must be aware that when you are found out, it could harm any possibility of you ever finding a suitor, or for that matter, a husband."

The corners of her lips quirked, and she waved away his comment. "I have no need for either. I have decided to remain at home with my parents and continue a life free of the constrictions that come with marriage."

For some reason disappointment gathered in him. It was as if he'd spied a beautiful bird dying and knowing the creature's songs would be silenced forever. "Do you really feel that way?"

Siobhan nodded, then appeared to sniff the air. She frowned. "I am sorry, my lord. I do wish I had time for tea, but your advice has reminded me that Henriette and I must hurry home. I am sure my mother and Amelia have plans for a ride or something 'appropriate' for a young, marriage-minded lady such as my sister. Although, hopefully, suitors will come for her, and she will be distracted from the plan to promenade." She made to walk past him and return to her carriage.

He was surprised to feel disappointed, and it occurred to him he wasn't saddened that they weren't going to share tea but because she was hurrying away from him. Why he was reluctant to allow her to leave, he could not—no, *would* not—say.

Miles had to fight the instinct to reach for her arm and ask her to stay with him a bit longer. After all, he reminded himself, he wasn't interested in any entanglement—though all of a sudden his reasons for declaring this weren't as clear as they'd once been. No matter. He shook himself. "I will walk you to your carriage then." After all, that was the gentlemanly thing to do and had nothing to do with the fact that he wanted to spend as much time as he could with her, stretching out every minute for as long as he could.

The carriage was but a few steps away and once there, he could finally touch her, as he assisted her onto the wooden stool the driver produced for the task, and then into the carriage.

He took her elbow as she lifted her skirts and stepped up. It was an informal touch. He'd helped many women get into carriages, so it startled him when it affected him, sending a jolt of something that sparked up his arm and across his chest to wrap around his heart. Thrown off balance by this reaction, he let his fingers linger on her arm just a bit too long. Siobhan's eyes swung to his, the ice blue pools taking him in. A slight crinkle formed between her brows. The moment was fleeting, but he could swear she, too, was surprised by whatever magnetic, unexpected physical reactions transpired between them.

"Enjoy the rest of your day, my lord," she said, her voice husky as it brushed his ears.

If the driver noticed anything, the man did not give it away; his expression was stoic as he closed the door and picked up the stool. Then the sturdy man touched his cap and tilted his head in a slight bow. "My lord."

Miles stepped back and onto the sidewalk as the carriage pulled away.

"Sir!" A man from the market waved both arms and then motioned to his horse, feasting on a display of apples. Several had been dislodged and were on the ground as the incorrigible beast had nosed through the carefully crafted pyramid of fruit, destroying it as it searched out the perfect one.

Running over to the stall, Miles grabbed the reins. He'd not realized he'd released them while helping Siobhan into the carriage. Or maybe before that. He'd lost track of himself because he'd been so focused on the intriguing, curious miss.

"I do apologize." Miles pulled out his purse and paid more than the amount the man asked for. "I will take all the ones on the ground as well."

The man's eyes widened when he counted the coins. "Of course, sir." He helped put the apples into a bag which Miles attached to his saddle before he mounted up and headed to his townhouse.

Thankfully there were no planned outings the following day, which meant Miles had time to work on his plans to amass the amount needed for the sponsorship of a ship on which he and his friends were collaborating. He'd wasted enough time and if he was to win the wager he'd set, he had little time left.

Once arriving at his townhouse in the pristine area of town, he dismounted and gave the groom instructions to cut another apple for the horse and to give a few apples to his other steed. The groom laughed when Miles told him what the horse had done, and he ended up joining in with mirth.

The fire in the hearth along with the light from several lanterns greeted him when he entered the house. It was mid-day, and he had no plans other than to review financial ledgers and prepare to meet with his father the following day. Most of the accounting was done; all that was needed was to write a brief report. Once that was completed, he could perhaps read.

"Would you care for tea, my lord?" Firtha the housekeeper asked, entering the room behind him with a bowl of water and a washcloth.

Miles dipped the cloth into the lemon-scented water and ran it over his face, neck, and both hands. "I would. Perhaps something light to eat."

He lowered to sit behind the desk and opened the ledger. The numbers swam across the paper, making little sense. As birdsong sounded, he looked out the window to find a pair of birds on a branch just outside. The tiny creatures sang their hearts out as if challenging each other in a contest. It reminded him of Siobhan and how she seemed to enjoy challenging him, which made him wonder what she was doing now. Was she out for a ride with her mother and sister as she'd thought she might be? It was a lovely day for that, he had to admit. Would she agree, he wondered. And, if she did…he didn't let himself finish that thought because he might end up talking himself out of his impulsive decision.

The housekeeper reentered, and he waved the tray away. "Please send the footman to tell the groom, I would like my other steed saddled at once."

"You are going out again?" Often the woman left off his title as she'd raised him from a bairn. When she did, he never corrected her.

"I am. Do you require anything?"

If she was surprised by his question, she didn't show it. Instead she studied the tray. "Eat first. Drink your tea. You have time. Otherwise, you may get a headache." Apparently, she was *still* raising him, a fact that warmed his heart instead of annoying him.

Miles nodded. "I will eat while my horse is prepared."

What Firtha said was a stark reminder of the ailment he suffered from that very few knew about. But the fact was, unpredictable and crippling headaches were the ever-present danger in his day-to-day life. Because of them, he'd acquired a reputation for being aloof, as they sometimes caused him to flee gatherings without explanation. He lived in fear of their occurrence, rarely accepted outings to the country.

They were one of the reasons he disliked balls and routs, and spent as much time as he could outside on the balconies and avoiding conversation. It wasn't all because he eschewed the idea of marriage; he had a physical reason, a flaw, and he didn't want to let it be known. The headaches struck without warning, though often they followed too much activity, bright lights, or loud noises and gatherings. Indeed, the last two headaches had happened after attending crowded, noisy balls.

Ever vigilant and the one person who knew him better than any other, Firtha had noticed that they occurred less—or at least, lessened in severity—when he ate consistently and slept well; of course, this made her increase her mothering. But for that, he was grateful, because what young man wanted to maintain an old man's lifestyle? She made sure he took care of himself, and as a result few other people besides his family knew about his affliction. It had been weeks since the last time he'd remained in his bedchamber for days, blind with pain.

So now, Miles ate everything on the plate and slowly sipped his tea. The liquid calmed him, and the warmth enveloped him, and he was confident he'd be without pain or worry.

THE PARK WAS teeming with people who'd taken advantage of the warm weather and gone out for a promenade. Carriages circled, couples strolled, and people on horseback rode side-by-side around the perimeter of the beautifully landscaped and plush gardens of the park.

Benches were deliberately set here and there, allowing for those wishing to rest to have shade and just enough privacy. Canopies were erected on the center lawn, under which families sat on colorful blankets drinking tea and taking in the sights.

It was all deliberate. A way to see and be seen for the genteel set. People used the experience for visiting and conversation. And gossip, of course. All under the guise of fresh air and wholesome activity.

Absently, Miles wondered if his mother and sister had some-how convinced his father to come out. Probably not. Otherwise, a message would have been sent to him to join them in a formal family outing.

"Lord Miles!" Glenora McIntyre, a wealthy widow, called from the grounds to his right. "Care to join me?"

As he neared the wealthy woman's canopy, his stomach sank. He'd considered seducing the woman in order to gain the capital for the ship, as Glenora was quite wealthy. In her forties, widowed, bored, and lonely, she remained very attractive. But suddenly, the idea of seducing the woman was not as appealing a proposition as it had been. She was suddenly too old, too jaded, and the idea of entertaining her now seemed unpleasant. Something had shifted in him, and he wasn't sure he liked it.

Still, he needed to be polite. Miles dismounted and after hand-ing the reins of his mount to one of her footmen, he strolled to greet her. "Lady McIntyre, it is nice to see you," Miles said, taking her proffered hand and kissing it. He then took her companions in. Two women and a man whom he'd met once or twice. After he'd made his salutations, Glenora invited him to join their party. If he changed his mind in order to win the wager and were to approach Glenora for money, he had to know what the woman would ask of him. At the moment, he had no desire to even try.

"I am looking for Mother," Miles said, not quite lying, though it was mostly an excuse to leave and search for Siobhan. So after he made his greetings, he gathered his horse from the footman and proceeded to walk along the path.

Such folly, to be so obsessed with the woman. He wasn't interested in pursuing a relationship with her, after all. But still, she was so intriguing woman, so unlike any other. She was always up to something unexpected, he decided. Who wouldn't want to know more? Her beauty and that peculiar tingle from when they'd touched had nothing to do with his interest. It was because of her unpredictability, her sense of humor, and her extraordinary kindness and willingness to help others less fortunate. So she wasn't just beautiful on the outside, she had a beautiful heart.

He mused about this as he walked. The pathway led him past several families who enjoyed extraordinary spreads while drinking sparkling champagne. He acknowledged several of them as expected, before noting whom he sought.

On a bench, holding parasols to hide them from the sun, were Amelia and her mother, who were speaking to another pair of women. Meanwhile Siobhan stood nearby in the bright sunshine. She was laughing as she threw pieces of bread to an aggressively quacking flock of ducks, who surrounded her and flapped their wings at one another.

He circled around to avoid walking in front of the others and came up to Siobhan's left.

At first she frowned, then smiled at him. Just seeing her smile made something stir in his chest. "Miss Blair. I am pleased to see you again so soon."

She hitched her chin and both her brows rose. "I told you they had planned an outing." Siobhan nodded in the direction of her sister and mother. "I must admit, it is a perfect day for it. Care to toss some crumbs?" She held out the basket of stale bread.

He reached for a handful and tossed it out across the water so the birds would move away. "I'm afraid my gray might stomp one," he admitted. "He really needs the exercise."

She gave a laugh, which was what he'd intended. "Well then, duck stomping might be a way to do it, though I daresay it is rather—"

"Lord Miles, what a pleasant surprise!" Amelia had gotten off the bench and moved to stand between them. When she slid a look to her sister, there was a silent message in her expression which Miles didn't quite understand.

It was obvious Siobhan did, because she narrowed her eyes. "Sister, Lord Miles was just telling me he brought his horse out to enjoy the beautiful weather—and to see the ducks." Her lips curved as she glanced quickly at him, sharing their joke.

Amelia barely glanced at the horse. "Lord Miles, you must know how happy I am to see you. We did not get much of an opportunity to speak the other night."

"Siobhan," their mother called out then. "Come sit with me for a moment. Get out of the sun."

There was no subtlety to what happened. Zinnia Blair wished for him and Amelia to be able to speak privately. Miles looked around, hoping to see someone to use as an excuse to leave. Unfortunately no one was near enough.

"Would you take me for a turn, my lord?" It was more of an order than a request. Courtesy demanded he comply, and he held his arm out.

They strolled around the pond away from Siobhan with him leading his horse behind them. "I am sure you have received plenty of requests from gentlemen since the season started." He began the conversation with what he hoped would lead to letting her know he was not interested in a relationship.

"You flatter me, my lord," Amelia replied, her eyes moving to him then back to the path in front of them. "There have been a few. I will take my time before deciding. I must admit to feeling disappointed you were not among the callers."

Miles assumed the most neutral expression he could. "It is

important you know that I am not interested in courting or marrying."

Amelia hesitated for a moment, her steps faltering. "Is that so? May I inquire why?"

He didn't owe this woman anything. Certainly not an explanation or reason for how he wished to live his life. "We should return. I cannot dally. I am supposed to be looking for my mother and sister."

Despite his statement, Amelia was not put off. "Of course, you will marry. You are your father's only heir. Upon his passing, you are to become the Duke of Spencer and must therefore produce an heir." Her stating the obvious in such an uncouth and uncaring manner annoyed him, and he took a breath to keep from telling the woman to mind her business.

"One day perhaps. But I doubt that will be for a few years, and it is certainly nothing to which I look forward."

The woman's face hardened, her jaw set, and her lips pressed into a tight line. It was a hard and calculating expression, and showed, he decided, how she differed from her sister, who would never focus on his title or point out how his father's death was something positive. "It is a pity you're not searching for your wife now, when the perfect women are available to you. You may lose out on obtaining their hand."

Although he was aware she was insinuating herself, Miles looked at where Siobhan now stood closer to the edge of the pond, apparently communing with her feathered friends. She was bending low and reaching out to them with wiggling fingers.

"I have been told that when the right person comes along, they have the power to change our mind," he said unintentionally.

Amelia tossed her head and snarled, "Indeed," as she looked at Siobhan, who now appeared to be studying the aquatic plants. Perhaps she sought frogs, or fish. It was hard to tell, with Siobhan, which of course made him want to leave this calculating miss to find out. And Amelia could tell he was inattentive to her wiles.

He wondered if she knew how ugly her narcissism made her, especially in comparison to her sister, a woman who was more concerned with the welfare of others than of her own reputation and desires. If only he truly was in the market for a wife. He knew exactly what kind of woman he would choose, and she was nothing like Amelia.

CHAPTER FOUR

H ER MOTHER AND sister were quite inept at keeping secrets or hiding anything from Siobhan. Since she'd been young, she'd always caught them when they'd tried to keep something from her. It was not only that their guilty expressions gave them away, but also apparently that they could not whisper.

On that particular afternoon, Siobhan noticed their absence from the sitting room. She'd then spied them in the arboretum, heads together, speaking in low tones. Every once in a while one or the other's head popped up and she'd scanned the room to make sure no one came upon them.

Siobhan ducked behind a large flowering bush to ensure they didn't see her and inched closer. Whatever they were in the midst of concocting, they wanted to keep from her, which could only mean trouble.

Amelia huffed. "Mother, I cannot just ask a man into the garden. It is the man who offers to escort."

"Listen to me," her mother whispered too loudly. "It is important that you get him to the garden when the second waltz begins. Come up with any excuse. Then, when you spot me and whoever I managed to get to walk out with me, fall against him."

Siobhan stopped herself from gasping aloud. They were plotting to compromise Miles! The plan was weak, but the gossips would make whatever occurred seem as if they'd walked in on two naked people in the middle of…whatever scandalous thing it was that naked people did.

"Fall against him," Amelia parroted. "Should I wrap my arms about him?"

"Even better," her mother replied enthusiastically. She popped her head up and searched the room before instructing, "Keep your voice down," although it was she who had spoken too loudly in her excitement that Amelia was coming around to the plan.

A tiny caterpillar caught Siobhan's attention and she followed the creature's path with her eyes while considering what to do about this. Why did her mother insist on Amelia marrying Lord Miles? Even a blind person could see that they were completely incompatible. Miles stiffened when Amelia neared and her sister, who usually had no problem in social situations, became awkward.

It was true that the man was indisputably one of the most handsome men in Glasgow. Not only that but one day, he would inherit his father's title and become the Duke of Spencer. And it was also true that the woman who married Lord Miles would become a duchess. These reasons alone created a rare and enticing motivation for any woman to attempt to seduce him. Or worse, trap him into marriage.

It was not to be borne. That decision made, Siobhan hurried past the many plants of the arboretum, and out to the corridor. Continuing to her father's study, she knocked, then entered before he could speak.

Her father lifted his head to look at her, quill held up. "Is something wrong, Siobhan?" A drop of ink fell off the quill and landed on the paper with a soft plop. He frowned down at it.

Instead of speaking right away, she sank into one of the plush chairs in front of the oversized desk at which her father sat, and scanned the room. Two large dark wooded bookcases flanked the big desk, filled with books and even parchments of every size. Every period in history was included in his vast collection.

"To whom are you writing?" Siobhan asked, peering at the new piece of paper he used to replace the ruined one.

His eyes lit up. "I am inviting Sir Edmond Walker to speak at the club. He is an expert on Ancient Egypt."

Her heart lightened at his excitement. "How very interesting. Perhaps then you can travel there with your historical gentlemen's group."

"We are called *historians*, Daughter. The Glasgow Historians." He motioned to a plaque he'd received from said group. "This is not a mere hobby."

"Of course not," Siobhan replied in what she hoped was a serious tone, though she wanted to smile. At that, she pushed back a lock of her hair and let out a sigh. "Father, I wish to ask you something and I hope you will be honest."

"What is it, dear?"

After a glance to the door to ensure her mother or sister did not lurk nearby, eavesdropping, she spoke, thinking about what she'd heard from her mother and sister. They were so focused on using any means possible to trick Lord Miles into marrying Amelia. It was wrong, and it seemed the worst kind of behavior. She wanted to ask Papa what he thought about it but surprised herself by blurting out, "Do you think I will ever marry?"

Her father's expression softened, and he put the quill down before he clasped his hands together. "Of course, you will. You're quite bonnie. I think it is only because you are spirited that a man has not declared himself."

Spirited. It was the word that was often used when describing her. Siobhan looked past her father to see a bird fly past the window. How she wished for wings of her own. "I am not sure I wish to marry at times. If only you'd allowed me to—"

"I could not allow you to marry him, Siobhan," her father said in a stern tone. "He was without merit of any type."

Although she understood why her father had fired the young man she'd been infatuated with, her heart ached at the thought of it. Gerard had worked for them as a footman, and at eighteen, she'd thought him the most beautiful boy ever.

They'd kissed in secret, and she'd spent countless hours

dreaming of a life with him. But when they'd been caught one night by Amelia, the consequences had been swift.

By the next morning Gerard was gone, and she'd been banished to her room. Siobhan had to be forced to attend a social event after that year, where she'd refused every offer of a dance, and had escaped outdoors where she'd fallen asleep under a bush. Claiming to have been mortified when a gardener had finally found her, her mother had been furious and confined her to the house for the rest of the season, which was fine with Siobhan, more of a reward than a punishment.

That year her mother had made excuses, telling people that Siobhan was ill to keep tongues at bay. However, her notable absence had brought rumors of impropriety on her part. Every single bachelor had been rumored to have ruined her. But the important thing—at least for her parents—was that no member of society even considered that she'd been involved with someone of what they'd considered a "lower" station.

Two years had passed since then and the gossips had moved on to other, newer scandals. Everyone seemed to have forgotten the events of her coming out season. At least, outwardly. But that "spirited" description still followed her.

"You should make more of an effort if you wish to find a husband," her father said, interrupting her thoughts. "You are of age to be married. But of course, I'm sure you know that already. So the thing is, you should make an effort to find a *suitable* husband."

Siobhan nodded, annoyed that Miles Johnstone came to mind immediately. "I suppose I can make more of an effort. If only all the so-called 'suitable' men didn't remind me of pampered toads it would be easier."

Her father chuckled. "You never cease to entertain me, lass."

Unexpectedly, her mother entered the room, without knocking. "I must speak to you, Siobhan," she said, and then, "You should not be bothering your father while he works. It is time for tea."

Siobhan rose then and followed her mother from her father's office, giving him a smile of thanks as she left. As she walked behind Mother, she mused about her parents' seemingly strange relationship. They were very different people and didn't appear to suit. And it was true that they never showed their affection in front of anyone. But to her, it was obvious they were in love.

Though her mother was social, and cared greatly about what others thought of her and her father preferred his own company, they were oddly well-suited, more like two halves of a completed whole than opposite sides of a circle. Siobhan knew that her mother admired her husband's intelligence and intellectual pursuits while he—often uncomfortable in social situations—appreciated that his wife could speak to anyone and always knew how to act in society. Still, Siobhan wondered if he knew that Mother was scheming to entrap a lord into marrying their daughter. Would he admire that?

A sudden thought occurred to her: Had Mother entrapped Papa? It wasn't impossible to believe, because how else would she ever have gotten the quiet, studious man to notice her? In Siobhan's estimation, he rarely set foot in a ballroom, either now or then.

It was an intriguing thought, though probably not a proper one.

Once they were seated in the sitting room, her mother poured tea. Amelia lounged nearby working on her most recent embroidery. Her gaze flitted from her and back to the hooped fabric in her hands.

Siobhan wanted to roll her eyes at Amelia's obvious attempt at inattention. Why even bother to pretend to embroider if she was going to be so focused on her, instead? She took a deep breath and forced herself to sip her tea while she waited for whatever schemes her mother and sister were planning to foist upon her. She had no doubt that while they were aiming to capture Lord Miles, the pair's plot included her somehow. Right now, they were putting their plan for her into play.

"I must state that your actions when around Lord Miles have been most inappropriate," her mother stated, then sipped the tea before deliberately placing the cup down. "Darling, you must not be so...*familiar* with men. They will get ideas."

"Such as?" Siobhan pretended innocence. "What kind of ideas, Mother?"

"Well..." Her mother's cheeks colored, and she picked up her cup again, using it to hide her face as she murmured, "That you are without regard for propriety."

What her mother stated was true. Since her father had sent Gerard away, she'd lost any desire to even pretend to enjoy the goings on of high society. "I do not seek them, or Lord Miles, especially, out. In fact, it is quite the opposite."

"Regardless, you must avoid him at all costs."

Siobhan was unable to keep from smiling. Her mother was so calculating, even in her actions with the cup. She was like an actress in a play, though she probably thought she was being quite clever. "Why? If he is interested in me, then he would make a suitable husband. Wouldn't you be proud that I could one day be a duchess?"

Her mother's eyes rounded, and she swallowed visibly before attempting a neutral expression. "I cannot picture that." It had always been obvious to everyone, except maybe her mother, that she favored Amelia. In Siobhan's estimation it was fair, as she herself took after her father, who doted on her in return.

Her mother's remark was not unexpected, and yet, it did smart. "Mother, you truly do not think I could hold a title and be a fine and proper duchess?"

Her mother frowned and waved her hand dismissively. "Do not jest, Siobhan. You are far too...*spirited* to be married to a duke."

That description, again? "I wish everyone would call me something other than 'spirited'. Why not troublesome, or mischievous, or even mad?"

Amelia stopped pretending not to be listening. "You *are* mad.

I do not understand why he would ever seek you out. You're everything a duchess isn't. What does he see in you?"

Siobhan took a deep breath, partially to appear calm instead of displaying the spirit they constantly accused her of showing, and partially because the thought of Miles seeking her out made her feel like flying. Did he seek her out? It had seemed that way to Siobhan, too, but she didn't want to believe it to be true. Yet, if Amelia and her mother noticed it, perhaps... She exhaled. "Perhaps it is because neither of us enjoys social events and both of us recognize we're seeking ways to avoid being there."

Amelia narrowed her eyes. Her mother shook her head. "He is obligated to attend events. His family holds an important place in society. Unlike you, who does not hide her disdain for gatherings, he performs his duties admirably."

"Are you his protector, Mother?" Siobhan asked. "Why the sudden interest in Lord Miles?" Perhaps she could get them to admit their plan.

Her mother glanced toward Amelia before admitting, "I believe your sister could gain his attention—if you stop interfering."

Before she could reply with something she'd regret, Siobhan bit the tip of her tongue. Despite that she didn't want to be married, and especially did not want to give up her freedom and her own pursuits as she would under the thumb of whoever she married, the idea of Miles with his sister turned her stomach. That he'd be present at family events, married to Amelia, brought on a sensation she'd never felt before. Her pulse quickened and her breath caught as a knot rose to her throat.

It was best to leave the room. When she got to her feet, her dress caught on the table, sending the teacups to clatter; one even tipped, splashing tea over the surface.

"You ask why I can't see you acting as a duchess, Siobhan? Goodness, your lack of decorum makes you simply unsuitable for any social gathering," her mother said, righting her cup and throwing a napkin over the spilled tea.

"I am tired of you acting as if I am unredeemable." Siobhan looked from her mother to her sister. "But you do not have to fear that I'm going to interfere with your plans to trap Lord Johnstone into marriage. I will not attend any more social events this season."

She ignored the astonished looks they exchanged and then gave her. Instead, she swept from the room, blinking away her tears.

"Siobhan!" her mother called after her, but she pretended not to hear.

HENRIETTE SHOOK HER head. "I cannot believe your mother chastised you in such a manner."

They were headed to a performance put on by a local string quartet. It was to be outdoors, and it was sure to be the perfect escape as her mother and sister did not plan to attend, citing the lack of adequate cover from the sun. Siobhan suspected it was more likely they would not attend because no one of note—in their estimation, anyway—was to be there.

It suited Siobhan just fine as the last thing she wished to do was to attend any event with them at the moment.

Upon arriving at the gates to the gathering, her mood lifted. Women in colorful afternoon gowns strolled the gardens and clustered about the refreshments served at beautifully decorated tables as they awaited for the announcement that the performance would begin. In another part of the garden, rows of chairs were arranged in a semi-circle which would allow everyone to see the performers. They were also arranged so that there was space for attendees to get up for additional refreshments or to converse during breaks. After acquiring beverages, Siobhan, Henriette, and Jean-Paul chose chairs at the end of a row.

As soon as the first bars of music flowed over them, Siobhan noticed Miles. He was escorting a woman to sit and then lowered to the chair beside her. Since the woman was wearing a wide-brimmed hat, she could not see who it was. However she could tell that the woman was elegantly dressed in a lavender gown, and that she had golden hair which spilled over her shoulders from beneath the head covering.

Henriette caught a glimpse of Lord Miles as well, and she jabbed an elbow into her side. "He's here with someone," her friend whispered.

"I noticed," Siobhan replied. "Who is she?"

"I think it is Glenora McIntyre," Henriette replied. "She is very wealthy, and somewhat older than we are. And older than Miles! I think she's a widow."

Because of Mother's interest in society gossip, Siobhan was familiar with the woman. Glenora was very lovely and, from what she'd heard, well-liked. However, at the moment, she herself was not inclined to like the woman. All interest in the entertainment faded as she watched the interaction between Miles and Glenora.

Every so often they spoke to each other, probably about the musical piece. For the most part, they remained attentive to the music, neither of them drinking nor eating anything.

Seeming to sense her watching, Miles turned in her direction. Before he caught her, she looked away, pretending she hadn't noticed him and most definitely that she wasn't watching his every move. Still, out of the corner of her eye, she could see his gaze lingering on her, and could even feel it; her skin tingled, and her heart pounded. Finally, however, the sensation left her and when she carefully peeked at him, he was speaking again to Glenora.

Once intermission arrived, Henriette stood. "The music is wonderful. It flows gently over us, touching every sense."

Jean-Paul gave his sister a droll look. "Poetry, dear sister?"

Henriette rolled her eyes and huffed. "I am stating what I feel."

"Well. *I* feel like going for a walk," Jean-Paul said, and hastened off to wander through the gardens. Siobhan suspected he'd seen a young lady he wished to pursue and was using the opportunity—and the privacy afforded by the topiaries—to meet her.

She wished she could walk through the garden too, though there was no one she wished to meet. Not anymore. Because the object of her desire was here with someone else. "I agree. The music was beautifully performed," Siobhan replied, still distracted and watching Miles and Glenora standing together, still talking. But then, a pair of women approached the couple and soon after, Miles walked away from the trio. Her heart began to pound as she realized he was heading in her direction.

"I will go fetch something to eat. I am famished." Before Henriette could insist on going with her, she hurried away toward a stall that she hoped sold something good. Hopefully he would not approach her. If word got to her mother that she'd defied her orders, she worried she might not be allowed on any more outings with Henriette for fear she'd ruin her plans to land a lord for Amelia.

But her hopes were thwarted as Miles caught up to her, arriving at her side. "Miss Blair, are you avoiding me?" His velvety voice seemed to wrap her in warmth like a cloak. "Perhaps you did not see my approach."

When she looked up at him, a smile played at the corner of his lips; he knew she was running away from him, and he was laughing about it! Her heart skipped a beat. Not only because he was teasing her—and obviously pursuing her—but also because, dressed in deep blue, he made a wickedly dashing picture.

Still, she tried to maintain an air of normalcy and not let him know how he affected her. "I am not, my Lord. I am famished, as I skipped morning meal." She motioned to the stand they'd approached.

"I see." He took her elbow and guided her to another stall. "You must be particularly famished. It seems to have affected your eyes, Miss Blair because if you're hungry then you should eat food, and not fans."

Her face warmed as she realized she'd been heading toward a stall that displayed fans for sale. She let him lead her to where a heavy-set woman sold honeyed oat cakes. Miles purchased three, and handed one to her.

Perhaps she really was too spirited, she thought, because she possessed none of the man-catching wiles her mother and sister seemed to have; it was impossible for her not to be forthright and express exactly what she was thinking. "Your companion may not take lightly to you speaking to me during intermission." Siobhan stole a glance in the direction where the woman continued in what seemed a lively conversation with her companions.

Miles lifted an eyebrow. "She asked for something sweet to eat." He shrugged as if unconcerned by the widow. "Are you planning to attend the Mackenzie's ball tomorrow night?"

Her heart soared even as her stomach fell. "I am not." She took a deep breath. "But since you are planning to attend, I must advise you to avoid the gardens."

His eyebrows rose, but she shook her head. She wouldn't reveal her mother and sister's plans. She had to remain loyal to her family, even as she disagreed with their tactics. "Thank you for the honey cake, my lord." With that, she swept around him and walked to meet Henriette.

But through the rest of the performance, Siobhan could not pay attention. Her mind kept returning to Miles and why he'd asked about her attending the ball. It was strange, but she could not shake the feeling that he'd seemed relieved and not disappointed when she'd said she would not be going. Or had she imagined it?

She could not help but worry about it. Was it possible that he planned to escort Glenora, and did not wish for Siobhan to be there and embarrass him in some manner? Did he, too, think she was too "spirited", like her mother and sister and practically everyone else? Her eyes narrowed in his direction just as he peered over at her.

Their eyes clashed. She kept her eyes narrowed in response to his questioning gaze. Why even bother? What did she care how he felt? It was of no consequence, not to her. It *could not* be of any consequence.

Siobhan gritted her teeth and looked away but the question of how he'd felt about her non-attendance to the ball plagued her. Had he been relieved? Was that the reason? Maybe it was because he did not wish for Glenora to know he and she were acquainted. If not for her mother's stern talk about impropriety, she would have bumped into them after the performance and ensured that Glenora became aware she and Miles were acquainted.

"Is something the matter?" Henriette asked, looking at her with concern. "You seem very cross."

Siobhan smiled. "I was thinking about what Mother said. I should put it out of my mind. However, it does annoy me," she admitted.

"You must not dwell on it," Henriette said. Her friend did not understand how much easier it was for her to say that than it was for Siobhan to do that—though she tried.

When the performance ended, two men approached and waited for them to acknowledge their presence.

Henriette's cheeks pinkened prettily. "Lord MacIntosh, I did not expect you'd be here."

Lord MacIntosh was of medium stature, handsome, and with vivid blue eyes. His attention was riveted on Henriette. Henriette introduced him to Siobhan.

His companion, a tall, dark brunette man with equally dark eyes stood by, waiting to be introduced. Lord MacIntosh motioned to his friend. "This is Charles Winthrop, recently returned from travel."

The man kissed both of their hands, but his scrutiny lingered on Siobhan. "I am pleased to make your acquaintance, Miss Blair."

Jean-Paul had yet to return, which meant he had probably

been distracted by a woman as Siobhan had suspected. Henriette didn't seem to mind one bit.

"May we escort you to your carriage?" Lord MacIntosh asked her friend, who nodded in agreement.

"Where did you travel?" Siobhan asked Winthrop, who walked beside her. By the way he kept stealing glances at her, it was apparent he found her attractive.

"On safari in Africa. I also went to Egypt and Morocco."

"My father is in the midst of coordinating a talk on ancient Egypt. Perhaps you could meet with him. He would be delighted to speak to someone who's been there recently. He's a historian interested in antiquities." She didn't mean the invitation as a way to get to know him better, though she worried it might sound that way. "He would genuinely be very intrigued with your travels," she added, just in case.

"If I may call on you tomorrow, I would be happy to speak to your father." Winthrop looked at Lord MacIntosh. "And perhaps a carriage ride after, with Thomas and your beautiful friend?"

It was all the encouragement both Lord MacIntosh and Henriette needed. Plans were made while Siobhan wanted to kick herself for encouraging the man into thinking she might be interested in him.

CHAPTER FIVE

T HE BALLROOM WAS crowded and overly hot. Miles made an
excuse to Glenora, who'd clung to his side for much too
long, and went out onto the balcony. The cool fresh air almost
made him close his eyes as it swept across his face like a lover's
caress.

He'd not escorted Glenora to the event, despite her obvious
hints, claiming the usual excuse of escorting his sister. But then
she'd run into him at the event and had been determined to
capture all his attention. As much as he should appreciate how
easy it would be to seduce the woman, the fact of the matter was,
he was not interested in her—or her money.

His three friends, Evan, Grant, and Henry had all acquired
the necessary funding for the sponsorship of the ship to the West
Indies through various means. Always wishing to win and despite
having enough money himself, he'd wagered that he'd come up
with the necessary funding in seven days by seducing a rich
widow. Glenora was making the wager far too simple and hardly
a wager at all.

Even though she was the key to gaining the money for the
sponsorship of the ship, the more time he spent with the woman,
the less he wished to seduce her. But never one to back down
from a challenge, he considered other ways to come up with the
money. He supposed he could just ask her for a loan, but then
rumors of his family having financial instability would spread.
Although it could be proven they were quite wealthy, rumors

would persist and in truth, it would involve his parents, something he truly did not want to do.

While looking at the stars in the darkened sky, he mused about other ways to come up with the funding. At first, the wager had been an entertainment for him and for his friends. But now it was nothing but a chore and in a few days, he would lose to Grant.

Maybe he could just give up.

"Lord Miles." Amelia Blair approached. "I find you have not signed my dance card as yet." She held up her card and pretended to study it, her eyes flitting from it to him. "Thank goodness there is one spot left."

As much as he wished to avoid dancing with the persistent young woman, propriety dictated he had little choice. Before taking the offered pencil, he searched the room for anyone who could rescue him. Of his male friends, only Grant was in attendance. At the moment, however, he was nowhere to be found. Across the huge ballroom, his mother and father stood too far to get their attention, although they would in all probability not try to help. For them, Miss Blair was considered an acceptable choice for a bride. He was trapped.

"Brother!" To his delight, Penelope seemed to appear out of nowhere. Even though he'd said she shouldn't attend any more balls, apparently she'd managed to override his wishes and now he was more than relieved of it. As far as he was concerned, right now especially, she could attend any balls she wished, if she could be relied on to get him out of dancing with persistent and unwanted misses. "I cannot find Mother. Have you seen her? Where is she?"

He wanted to grab his sister and hug her. "I will help you find her." He acted as if he'd forgotten about the pencil and the dance card, and bowed his head to Amelia. "If you will excuse us…"

Penelope pulled his arm as he practically dragged her back into the ballroom. "Slow down. You act as if there's a fire behind us." Her face was bright with mischief. "I could tell that you wished for help. So I came."

Miles laughed and touched the tip of her nose with his finger. "I adore you."

"I know." She laughed.

He began leading her toward their parents, but Penelope apparently had other plans and began to tug him toward a corridor. "Now, you must help me." Her heart-shaped face became serious. "A man is following Corrine and me non-stop. I declined his offer to sign my dance card, but he did it anyway. I do not wish to tell Father because he will only state that I should be polite."

"Who is this man?" He knew that was not the case; if their father learned what type of man this was, he would do whatever he had to in order to protect Penelope. Still, Miles had to force his hands to unclench.

Penelope motioned to a man who stood with two others and Miles frowned. He was well aware of the pompous man. He was called Tom Roberts, son to a very wealthy woman and much too old for his young sister. Not only that, but Miles had learned from Grant that Roberts had a penchant for what he would call the "darker side of sexual relations".

The man was the last person he'd ever allow near his sister.

"Do not worry. It is taken care of. Where is Corinne?" He peered down at his sister.

"She's hiding behind the plant there." Penelope pointed out her young friend, who lingered behind a huge potted tree, watching the people on the dance floor. Her feet moved to the music, but she wisely remained hidden behind the pot. In truth, even though it veiled her from the view of most of the people in the ballroom, it wasn't a very good hiding place. That being said, Miles knew that once Roberts spotted her, it might become a dangerous spot where he could accost her and no one would be the wiser.

"Come," Miles took his sister's hand and together they went to where Corinne was. Once he gathered both girls, he took them to sit in an alcove behind his parents.

His mother gave him a quizzical look. "They should be out there enjoying the evening, not sitting behind us."

Miles walked to stand between his parents. "Father, you know the man named Tom Roberts, I believe. He has made the girls...*uncomfortable* with his attentions. I will speak to him. Until then, they should remain here."

"There is nothing wrong with a man showing interest," his mother stated.

His father, however, slid a look to where Roberts stood. "Please do. Else, I will."

When his mother looked at them, the duke spoke to her in a quiet tone. "He has inherited his mother's tastes when it comes to...*entertainment*."

The duchesses' eyes rounded and then narrowed. "Miles, please warn him off immediately."

He nodded and bowed, then moved to the edge of the dance floor, where he waited while Roberts danced.

"Dance with me," Glenora said, coming to stand next to him. With little choice in the matter, he guided her to the dance floor. She, of course, knew Roberts as well—probably too well, if Grant's information was correct—and Miles had no doubt she would interfere in some way, possibly making the situation worse.

As they danced, he noticed Amelia and her mother watching. He'd not signed her dance card, and she'd said it was full except for one dance, so why wasn't she on the dance floor with someone else? Clearly, he was her prey, and she was husband-hunting. He wondered why the young woman had set her eyes on him over any other bachelor. The fact of the matter was, she was eye-catching, and surely suitors were calling. But she appeared undeterred.

He had explained to her that he had no plans whatsoever to court anyone. Perhaps he would reiterate it to her again tonight and set things straight.

The dance ended, and he escorted Glenora back to where she and her friends had congregated. "I will return shortly. I must speak to someone."

"Of course." She gave him a questioning look but said nothing else. In the meantime, Roberts had walked in the direction of where his sister and her friend were seated when Miles caught up with him.

"A word, Tom." Miles did not wait for a reply. Instead he walked out to the garden, after making sure the man was following. It was best to speak outdoors so as not to be overheard. The last thing he wanted was to make a scene and cause his mother any distress or his sister and her friend any embarrassment.

He finally stopped at a distance where he was sure, would be out of gossips' earshot, on the grass between some topiaries. Roberts caught up with him.

"What can I do for you, my lord?" Tom Roberts' eyes were dull, unfocused. He'd probably partaken in opium, by the slowness of his words.

"I will be blunt," Miles started, hoping the drugged man would hear him clearly. "You are to stay away from my sister and her friend. Do not speak to them. In fact do not dare to even look at them. Am I clear?"

The man's lips twisted into a sneer. "You can't order me about. You are no one. Am *I* clear?" he retorted.

It was only when Miles moved closer, until they were nose to nose, that Roberts seemed to regret his statement.

Miles narrowed his eyes, pinning the man's with his. "You are bothering my sister and her friend. Therefore, I have every right to order you to leave them alone. You do not want to cross me, Roberts. I asked courteously this time. I would advise against me having to remind you less politely next time."

The man backed away, his stance suddenly stronger and focus clearer, if only for the moment. "I only asked for a dance. I have no need to chase after children." He turned and stalked away, back into the ballroom.

"Lord Miles!" Amelia's voice cut through the darkness and the blonde came into view.

Miles cursed under his breath, suddenly remembering Siobhan's warning to avoid the garden tonight. And now, he knew why.

"Miss Blair," he replied. A new song played, this time a waltz. It was the second waltz, which meant the night would hopefully come to an end soon. "If you would excuse me. I do not wish to compromise you by being seen alone with you," Miles said, taking a step away.

The woman perked up, listening to the music. She walked around him, blocking his path. "May I ask you something before you go?" She blinked rapidly as if trying to think of something, her eyes flitting past him. "Oh! I feel a bit faint."

He stepped back instead of toward her as she most likely expected and looked at the house. How far away was it, and were there any people around to whom he could appeal to avoid being trapped in a compromising position? Unaware, apparently, that he was wise to her wiles, she collapsed toward him, probably expecting him to catch her. Predictably, the woman fell forward but since he wasn't willing to catch her, she landed face first with a soft thud and lay sprawled on the grass. "Oh!" she spluttered, her face covered in blades of grass and soft garden soil. Her cry alerted three women gathered at a nearby fountain and they rushed to her with exclamations of worry seemingly encouraging her to wail. Or perhaps she cried because her entrapment plans were foiled.

Miles had to swallow to keep from laughing. "Are you quite all right, Miss Blair?"

"Do not just stand there, help my daughter up," Zinnia Blair appeared now, running to Amelia, who seemed dazed. "What happened?"

"I tripped," Amelia replied lamely. "I took a step away from him when I saw you coming and stumbled."

One of the other women frowned at Amelia. "Dear, you must have hit your head. I clearly saw you fall forward. Lord Miles was looking away from you and didn't see you falling."

"Oh." Amelia gave her mother an alarmed look. "It is that…I suppose that could have happened. I-I mean, it was because we had been embracing and did not wish to be caught when we spotted these ladies nearby."

Her lies were transparent and pathetic. Suddenly, Miles was tired of this pursuit and no longer felt the need to remain polite. "We did not and have *never* embraced, Miss Blair," he said in as bland a tone as he could manage. "You should find yourself some water and a washcloth." He turned on his heel and stormed off.

He would speak to Siobhan and find out exactly what she knew about this. He'd always been adept at avoiding any kind of entrapment, usually escaping any woman out to ensnare him whether by seduction or by putting him in a situation that could be contrived as compromising.

This attempt had been less than well-planned or well executed and there was no doubt that Amelia Blair and her mother, although scheming, were not well-practiced. Once they were, he pitied whomever she set her sights on next.

WHEN SIOBHAN HEARD the sounds of horses outside, it took all her strength not to jump from where she sat and rush to the door.

Her father looked up from the book he read. After eating dinner, he'd joined her in the sitting room where he'd spent what was probably a peaceful evening—for him—of reading in front of a fire. He'd only been mildly interested in her reason for staying in and had not questioned her.

There were voices in the foyer as the butler greeted her mother and sister. Moments later, her mother entered the sitting room. Amelia walked past the doorway, presumably making her way to her bedchamber.

"Amelia is quite tired," her mother offered, although no one had asked.

"Did you enjoy your evening, dear?" Her father set his book on the arm of his chair and stood to move to her where he kissed her temple, then went to the sideboard. "Brandy?"

"Please," her mother replied. She slid a look to Siobhan. "It is late. You should be in bed."

"It is only just eight, Mama," Siobhan replied. "It is just that you have come home very early."

For a moment her mother seemed stunned, then she whirled to look at the clock. "So it is! Goodness, I thought it was much later." She accepted the drink from her husband, who settled onto the settee beside her. She turned to him. "Owen, you should have been there. The music was fabulous, the food, extraordinary. I must admit that the Edwina Mackenzie is well-versed in choosing the menu for her entertainments."

While her mother extolled the wonders of the evening, Siobhan noted she avoided any talk of those attending. When she could not wait any longer, she asked, "Did Amelia dance with Lord Miles?"

Her mother's eyes snapped to her. "I am sure she did."

"That's nice," she fibbed. "Did they walk in the garden?"

Her mother's eyes narrowed. "No, they did not. Honestly, Siobhan, I do not wish to discuss the evening's events."

So they'd failed, she decided. If they'd been successful in compromising Lord Miles, she would have been talking about nothing else. She exchanged an amused look with her father because in spite of the fact she wasn't discussing Lord Miles, the ball itself was all her mother had spoken about since entering the room.

Her father knew how to deflect his wife's moods. "What are your plans for tomorrow?" Siobhan almost giggled when her mother began telling him of her plans and he looked over to wink at her.

It wasn't until the next morning that her suspicions of their failed triumph were confirmed. Siobhan and her father had just begun eating when her sister entered the dining room. Amelia was in a sour mood, her lips downturned, face expressionless. There was a scratch across the tip of her nose.

After serving herself eggs and toast from the sideboard, her sister sat across from her. Siobhan poured tea for both of them. "You seem upset. Is something wrong? What happened to your nose?"

"I fell." Amelia let out a long sigh.

Their father's eyebrows rose as he peered over the edge of his coffee cup. "Whatever happened?"

Encouraged by the attention, she continued, though slowly to allow time for their gazes to linger on her. Amelia took a dainty sip of tea, then announced, "I tripped. It was horrifying. Lord Miles was there, but he made no attempt to catch me."

Siobhan could not control what happened next. When attempting to keep from laughing, food spewed from her mouth and across the table. Coughing when accidentally swallowing bits, she fought to catch her breath.

Her father stood and pounded her back none-to-gently until she finally stopped. "Are you all right?"

Her hand shook when she reached for the teacup and drank all the contents down. "I am truly sorry, Amelia." She tried to sound sympathetic, but was certain she had failed.

This was confirmed when Amelia pushed her food splattered plate away, and gave her a narrow-eyed look. "Did you laugh?"

Siobhan got up and filled two new plates with eggs, toast, and slices of cheese, sliding one in front of Amelia. "I did not. I choked."

Their father, the caring soul, studied Amelia. "Did you injure yourself badly, dear?"

Once more garnering attention, her sister's face turned from suspicious to full of dismay. "I did! I scratched my nose a bit, and my knees. Thankfully Mother was near, and she helped me to stand. While the dreadful Lord Miles walked away, not bothering to find out if I was injured."

There was silence and Siobhan looked from Amelia to her father. The sweet man looked at his daughter with concern in his eyes. "I am so sorry for your fretful time, darling."

Siobhan refilled her teacup. "So that is why you came home early."

"My gown was stained and hair disheveled. I lost the butterfly pin that I'd put in it," Amelia nearly wailed.

To Amelia's dismay their father could not hold back and chuckled. "I am sorry, but you must have presented a comical picture." When Amelia glared, he held up a hand. "I am glad you are not injured, dear one."

"You should speak to the horrible man and take him to task for allowing me to fall." Amelia pinned their father with dewy eyes. "Say you will." She blinked to make the show complete.

Siobhan turned away from them and rolled her eyes. Her sister's performance was almost good enough for the theater. But her father didn't appear to recognize her attempts to manipulate the situation. Instead, he proceeded to place some eggs and meat on his toast before cutting a bit to eat. "Next I see him, I certainly will," he agreed, and waved his fork.

LATER THAT MORNING, Siobhan could hardly wait to tell Henriette what had occurred. Unfortunately, upon arriving at her friend's house, her butler informed Siobhan that Henriette and Jean-Paul had gone to visit a sick aunt and had not yet returned.

"Would you prefer to return home, Miss? I do not think it would be safe for you to go to the market and such alone," the driver said as he helped her back into the carriage. "I will tell the man to have Miss Henriette send word when she is back from her visit. It will be safer."

But Siobhan knew the children were waiting and the idea that they were hungry hung like a cloud over her head. She could not delay her visit. Nor would she risk the chance that they wouldn't be fed that week, for who knew for what reason and for how long Henriette would be delayed? "Please have him tell Miss Henriette and her brother that they can deliver the items to the shelter at their convenience, but I will make our other, usual stop," she told the driver and he hurried to pass her message along to the butler before the carriage got on the way.

While she rode alone, her mind wandered to the night before. Despite her warning, Miles had gone to the garden with Amelia. Either that, or her sister had followed him out. Still, it seemed he'd avoided being ensnared by her mother's not-so-carefully formulated plan.

Perhaps her mother and Amelia would set their sights on someone else. Especially now that Amelia had apparently developed a strong dislike for him after he'd let her fall.

She frowned to herself. She didn't know Lord Miles well, but it was inconceivable to her that he would allow a woman to fall. He didn't appear to be uncareful or uncaring. He had been most kind when she'd taken her fall into him, which was more public and certainly more embarrassing.

So she had to assume it was Amelia who was at fault; she must have tried too hard upon seeing their mother approaching. It occurred to her that now *all* of society would gossip about how clumsy the Blair sisters were. Her mother had always blamed her for being a public spectacle, so it was ironic that her favored daughter would be the one to cement their reputation for a lack of grace. Her mother should have come up with a better strategy. Siobhan would almost appreciate the humor of it, if it wasn't going to cause such a bad look good for the family.

The carriage pulled to a stop with a jerk. In a moment, the

driver was at the door. "We are here, Miss," he announced as he opened the door to assist her. She reached for her market basket and climbed down.

Once in the market, she was lost in a sensory experience. The aromatic scent of fresh fruit intermingled with the heady aroma of tea and other spices. The almost-melodic voices of vendors who called out while displaying their offerings for passersby to inspect layered, one over the other.

People mingled, moving from one space to the other, reaching for items, haggling with merchants, and then paying. The music of the marketplace was further enriched by the jingling of coins, the shrieks of children at play, and the murmurs of groups of men standing idly by waiting for wives, sisters, or mothers.

After choosing some candies for the children, Siobhan added fruit and several loaves of bread from the nearby bakery to her basket. The driver hurried over to take it from her and walked with her to the building entrance.

"Go visit your family. I will be a bit since I have to help her bathe and see that the children are fed," Siobhan told the driver who looked up at the building and wrinkled his nose.

The man seemed reluctant when handing her the basket. "I do not know, Miss. I can visit with my mother another day. I'd feel better if I remained here with the carriage until you return."

"Nonsense," she said, waving her hand dismissively. "Your mother looks forward to your visits. She's elderly, and she needs to see you. I'll be fine."

He frowned and shifted, looking at his boots before he lifted his face to hers. "Okay, Miss. I'm going to leave the carriage here today, but I will not be long. Please ensure that you do not go anywhere. Please, wait for me here, in the carriage. I do not plan to be longer than you. Once I have helped you with the water, I will hurry to meet my mother."

He stood waiting as she went inside and climbed the stairs to the widow's apartment. As usual, she received a chaotic welcome from the excited trio of children. She got Emily to help with bringing in the water enough to fill the small tub, and she set it on the small stove to heat.

Susan seemed in good spirits, her soft eyes tracking the children as she told Siobhan about the past days. "The doctor you sent came by and prescribed medication. I am feeling better. I do believe I am regaining my strength." She waved to a neatly folded pile of clothing. "I was able to mend some clothes. It has been a long time since I was able to do so."

"That is wonderful to hear!" Siobhan felt encouraged that their efforts were showing positive results. Perhaps Susan would recover, and the little family would be saved. She continued to chat with the widow while completing as much of the cleaning and cooking as she could. After helping them to bathe and emptying the tub, Siobhan bid the family farewell and headed down the stairs.

"Miss?" A husky voice called from a dark corner of the stairwell. "A pence?"

Siobhan ignored him, hurrying to go the last few steps faster. An unusual sense of panic engulfed her. It was not typical for anyone to beg inside the building.

"Miss." The man moved closer, raising her already high sense of panic.

Sure he would continue to follow her, she prayed Ian was at the carriage. She pushed past the front door and out into the street, blind with fear. It was then that she realized she'd turned the wrong way and had gone to the back of the building, not the front.

A different man stood outside, seeming to fix the bridle on a large horse. He turned his head as she stumbled into the alleyway, his eyes narrowing.

Siobhan turned to the right, intent on rounding the building only to realize the pathway was blocked by a wall of refuse and barrels. She gasped, her throat seeming to close from the pounding of her heart, and she gulped for air. She turned again, and this time she saw the man had left his horse and was moving toward her, reaching for her. Suddenly, she found she was able to inhale a deep breath that escaped on a scream.

"No one is chasing you, Miss," said the man blocking her path. "Do not worry. I can escort you to wherever you wish."

She sidestepped away from his reaching hands. This *could not* be happening! "There is no need, my driver awaits."

The man nodded but continued moving toward her. "The best way to get to the front is to go through the building," he said motioning to the door.

Unfortunately what he said was true. Despite the fact the other man was still inside, she had little choice but to walk through the building. "Can you walk with me to my driver?" she asked, hoping to have chosen the lesser evil of the two.

The man nodded, giving her a smile that didn't reach his eyes. She still felt unsure, but what choice did she have? He was so much bigger than she and maybe she was just being fearful. Maybe he was willing to help her. "I'll be happy to walk you to your driver, Miss."

She turned. But then, she felt a tremendous shove, and she lost her footing. With a solid thump, her knees caught the brunt of the fall, the pain of their contact with the hard ground jolting through her in a blinding flash.

Just as she went to get up, she saw the other man leave the building and the two men pressed her to the ground, bound her hands behind her back and shoved a foul gag into her mouth. A meaty hand held it firmly in place.

When they pulled her to her feet, Siobhan fought like a wild beast, fear fueling her with strength. She managed to land a swift kick to one of the men's shins, and wrested free to run a short distance before she was grabbed and yanked back by her hair. Stars burst in her vision and her eyes watered from the pain. Quickly, one of the men tied her legs together at the ankles so she could not kick and the other lifted her like a sack of coal over his shoulder. She tried to struggle but it was of no use. She was helpless.

It was only when hauled, stomach down and hanging over the back of the horse the man had been standing beside that she realized in just how much trouble she was. Not only had she been attacked, but no one had witnessed it. No one knew who'd taken her, and in fact, no one knew she'd been taken. And then the situation grew worse, as a blanket was draped around her. It covered her head and face, and quite disguised her. She might as well have been a sack of coal for all anyone knew. There in the darkness and unable to move or cry out, Siobhan knew nothing but despair.

CHAPTER SIX

MILES HOPED TO find Siobhan and her French friend in the market. He had to talk to her and find out exactly what her mother and sister were up to. If the two had a plan to trap him, then it was best to know the particulars.

It didn't take long for him to realize she was not in the market as her almost-black, glossy hair was hard to miss. Besides, with their clear, clean skin and soft, white hands, the two women stood out as genteel, despite their "disguise" of older, serviceable clothing.

Perhaps he'd missed them, and they were now at the other building. He urged his horse forward, stopping when he spotted her family's carriage. Neither the driver nor Siobhan were anywhere in sight.

Curious, he neared the carriage and peered inside. It was empty. He would have to wait for her to emerge. Perhaps the driver had gone to find something to eat; surely the man would not be long in returning.

Just then a small boy burst from the building and raced to the carriage. Eyes wide, he looked up to the driver's seat and then circled the horses and peered from one side of the street to the other. It was clear from his tear-streaked face and frantic demeanor that he was searching for someone or something, and especially, that something was wrong.

Miles dismounted. "Are you looking for someone? Can I help you?"

"Where is the driver?" the boy asked.

"He is gone." Siobhan would need to know that her driver was gone; she shouldn't be leaving the tenement and emerging into the street alone and without a man's protection. But something in the boy's face—fear, maybe, or perhaps something frantic in his eyes—gave him an idea that she wasn't inside. "Do you know Miss Blair?"

The boy frowned. "Who?"

"Siobhan."

He started. "That's why I'm looking for her driver. He needs to know. The man took her." He pointed a small finger to the building. "A man stole Miss Siobhan." His bottom lip quivered. "We saw it from the window."

A sharp pang stabbed Miles' chest and his stomach seemed to fall. "What happened?"

The boy was crying now, heavy tears streaking down his face as his nose reddened, and he sniffed loudly. "She was fighting two men. They tied her and covered her with a blanket and put her over a horse. One of them got up behind her and rode away." The little boy pointed. "They went down the back-alley way."

Miles quickly mounted his own horse and gathered the reins. "Remain here. When the driver returns, tell him what happened. Tell him Lord Miles has gone after her."

Not waiting for a reply, he urged his horse to a gallop, rounding the building and heading down the narrow, garbage strewn street toward the part of town women like Siobhan should never know existed.

But where had they taken her? He should have asked more questions of the boy. What direction, exactly? What did the horse look like? What had she been wearing? What did they look like? If there were two men, did one of them walk while the other rode? Did they stay together? Were they separate?

He was a fool. He cursed himself, but didn't want to circle back to ask. Instead, he hoped he'd just find her and get her back to safety.

Up and down different streets he raced, without seeing any sign of her. The entire time, he prayed nothing sinister had befallen the beautiful woman. Leaning forward, he searched each alleyway and building enclave for signs of her or the man or men who'd taken her.

He was becoming disheartened when a scream tore through the air. *Please, God, let it be Siobhan.* As much as he didn't want her to need to scream, in reality it was the only way he'd find her.

His heart thumping against his breastbone, Miles whirled his horse in the direction the scream had come from and several moments later he finally caught sight of the other horse.

Atop a horse that was better suited for pulling a wagon, a man held a woman wrapped in a blanket against his body as they raced down a narrow street. The blanket had shifted, and her feet protruded from beneath it. He could see that she'd been tied at the ankles, and now was flopping like a fish in the man's grasp, her toes thumping the horse's shoulder. As he grew closer, he could see the other side of the blanket shifting and falling, and finally, he could see the top of her head and that beautiful, glossy black hair. A few people peered out the windows, but no one came out to help.

Mentally he prayed she'd not tumble from the horse; the fall could seriously cause harm, especially if the horse managed to kick her.

Once again she began screaming, the sound of it fueling his rage. He was still far behind, but his quick riding horse was closing the distance; the draft horse the man rode lumbered steadily but slowly and was no match for Miles' sleek thoroughbred.

He appeared to be pushing his hand under the blanket and withdrew it with a yelp as if he'd been bitten. "Ow! Ye foul wench. Keep that gag in yer mouth and stop yer struggling."

The screaming stopped. But so had the struggling. Was she all right? Heart in his throat, Miles dug his heels into his horse's side and the sensitive animal responded with a burst of speed, quickly gaining on the horse better suited for plowing a field or pulling a turnip wagon.

He glared at the startled man. "Stop at once!"

The man was obviously surprised at his presence, his rounded eyes taking him in. Instead of stopping, the idiot shook his head. "Go away. This woman…she is…She is my unmanageable wife."

The woman under the blanket gave an especially violent movement and it fell open, revealing Siobhan's face and her wide eyes. Siobhan worked her jaw and the cloth between her lips fell away as she spit it out, reminding Miles so much of an angry cat, it was hard not to smile. Or maybe he felt that way because of the relief flooding his system. "I should bite you again." She glared over her shoulder at the man. "Let me go!"

"I know the lady. She is not your wife!" Miles leaned over and attempted to grab the reins. The man fought to keep a hold on Siobhan while managing his quickly-slowing horse.

Despite the man's frantically thumping his heels in the big animal's sides, it ignored him and drew to a stop with a great sigh. Then it shook its huge head and yawned, flicking its ears and tail as if swishing away flies. Not meant for riding and not especially well-trained, the animal nickered to Miles' horse and shuffled its giant hooves on the pavement, refusing to budge even when the man kicked his heels into its sides.

"Release her," Miles instructed. "I will not ask again."

Face twisted in anger, the man threw Siobhan to the ground. His horse, startled by the rapid movement and flying blanket edges leapt ahead in surprise, nearly unseating the man. The big animal moved away at a gallop instead of its previous shuddering trot and the man became partially unseated. He desperately clung to its mane, shouting, "Whoa, y' daft beast!" The horse rounded the corner of a building, and the man flew into the other direction with a wail. But his fate did not concern Miles at the moment. What did concern him was Siobhan's sudden and uncharacteristic silence.

He slid off his horse and hurried to her to find that the fall had knocked her unconscious. He felt for a pulse and found it, relief flooding to every part of his body. He made quick work of untying her hands and ankles, then lifted her in his arms, with her head resting on his shoulder. Her hair brushed his cheek and a faint scent of violets rose to his nostrils. He hadn't even realized she smelled of violets; he hadn't held her close before. Now he would never be able to smell violets again without thinking of Siobhan. If he hadn't found her, he might have lost her.

Relief at having found her mixed with worry that she'd hit her head too hard. The fiery beauty was too quiet, and the serenity in her face was the kind only a complete lack of consciousness could bring.

Miles heard a carriage approaching and looked up to see it was the Blair family's conveyance. He wasn't sure how the man had found them and truly didn't care; the only important thing was that he was here.

The driver pulled the horses to a stop and jumped from his seat to rush to them. "I collared that other fellow until he gave me an idea of where she was being taken. I'm glad you found her, my lord." The man looked at Siobhan, and as he noted her stillness, the color drained from his face, leaving him pale.

It wasn't enough of a reaction for Miles. He fought fury to maintain his composure—the man should never have left Siobhan alone; if he'd been in Miles' employ, he would have terminated him immediately. As it was, he was too angry to trust what he'd say to the man. Instead, Miles motioned with his head to the horse. "Help me."

The carriage would have been better but there was no way he was going to allow her out of his sight, or his arms. From now on, she was under his protection. God forbid the man return and manage to snatch her out of the carriage somehow. Even if it was unlikely, there was a risk.

It was cumbersome, but with the driver's help, Miles managed to mount and hold her in his arms. After looking around, he finally gauged that they were much closer to his townhouse than her own.

When they arrived at his home, the entire staff came to life. The frantic and apologetic driver was quickly dispatched to notify Siobhan's parents and a message was sent to the doctor.

Miles carried her to his bedroom as the guest room was not as comfortable. His housekeeper washed Siobhan's face with a cool cloth. She'd yet to come to and it was worrisome.

"She should have awakened by now," Miles stated.

Firtha nodded and frowned. "The poor lass must have hit her head hard."

Miles thought about how she'd fallen. "It seemed to me she fell on her side, not on her head."

"I am sure the doctor will know what to do." The woman gave him a worried look. "I will bring you some hot tea with extra honey." With that she hurried from the room. A moment later, Miles realized he'd rather have whiskey, but did not wish to leave Siobhan alone for even a second until the doctor arrived.

Finally the housekeeper returned with a tray with a cup of tea accompanied by a glass of amber liquid.

"Bless you Firtha, you are truly a godsend." Miles gulped down the whiskey, ignoring the tea until the older woman gave him a pointed look. "For the nerves."

He reluctantly released Siobhan's hand and drank the overly sweet liquid.

It seemed an eternity before the doctor finally arrived. The man who'd seen to him for as long as Miles could remember gave him a curious look at seeing the beautiful woman in his bed. "Should I ask?" Then he put his bag down and began pulling out items.

Miles explained, "I thwarted her kidnapping. Her name is Siobhan Blair—"

"I know who she is," the doctor interrupted. "Her father and I are members of the Glasgow Historians."

Not sure what to make of that, Miles did not budge from his seat. The doctor began his assessment, then looked at him and asked if he planned to remain.

"I will. Unless you have to undress her."

The doctor shook his head. "No. Usually losing consciousness comes from a hit to the head. Explain to me what happened."

Again he repeated the story, the doctor listening intently whilst running his finger through Siobhan's hair. For an inexplicable reason, the act annoyed Miles. He followed the progress as the doctor carefully removed the pins from her ebony tresses and continued his examination.

"Ah," the physician said, holding up bloody fingers. Miles' stomach fell and he felt a bit woozy. She'd been more badly hurt than he'd realized. The question was—was she going to be all right? He'd never forgive himself if the vibrant, spirited young woman didn't recover.

"There is a gash to the back of her head," the doctor mused aloud as he inspected the wound. "But it is not what caused her to become unconscious. It is not deep and actually…it appears to be from the comb in her hair. It must have happened when she was first attacked."

"She was conscious and fighting when I caught up to them." Miles stood to help the doctor move Siobhan to her side.

"Fear and anger will sometimes propel a person to remain alert. The second fall and perhaps knowing you were there to rescue her allowed her body to finally succumb to the stress of the situation."

The pillow was covered with blossoms of red stains and, as Miles looked down at his coat he realized he, too, was covered in blood. Because he wore black, it had not been obvious at first. He'd been too overwhelmed with what occurred to notice.

"I best change before her parents arrive," he said, walking to the wardrobe to remove his coat.

Just as he walked out of the guest room after washing up and changing, knocks sounded on the front door. The butler opened to Amelia, her mother, and a stone-faced man he knew to be Owen Blair.

"She is being seen to by the doctor. It is best you wait until he finishes." Miles led them to the parlor where Firtha served brandy and offered sweetened tea.

Siobhan's mother began asking questions, one after the other, barely giving him time to respond. "How did you know Siobhan was in trouble? Who informed you? Who took her? Why?"

"Allow the man to answer you," Mr. Blair said, looking at Miles. And then he explained, "My wife is beside herself with worry as you can imagine. When the driver returned to tell us our daughter had been abducted and then rescued, we immediately went to see the constable."

Miles retold the sequence of events, noting that Amelia sat back looking around the room, taking in the walls and furniture, not seeming to listen to what he was saying. When she did look at him, she glared.

"It was a miracle that you happened to be in the same area," Siobhan's mother said wiping tears from her eyes. "Truly a miracle."

Miles had left out the part of going in search of Siobhan, stating instead that he was riding past on his way to visit a sick member of his staff. It was true several members of his staff lived in the area, but he'd lied about the illness.

"Did you recognize the abductor?" Mr. Blair asked.

"No," Miles replied, shaking his head. "I believe it was a matter of opportunity. Perhaps I am wrong. The man claimed that Siobhan was his wife. When I told him I knew her, then he pushed her off the horse."

Zinnia Blair gasped. "The low life scoundrel must be made to pay."

"I will speak to the constable and give a description," Miles stated just as the doctor entered.

Everyone got to their feet, except for Amelia, who looked on from where she sat.

"Mr. Blair, Mrs. Blair," he greeted them. "I am afraid Siobhan is still unconscious but there is little I can do but recommend complete rest. She must not be moved, and must remain where she is."

Both parents asked to be taken to see her. Amelia followed behind as the doctor led them to the bedchamber.

Miles lowered into a chair, wondering what would happen next. What an unexpected turn of events! He tried to fight back the panic that gnawed at him as again he wondered what he'd do if Siobhan didn't recover.

The doctor returned to the front room and motioned to the bar cart. Miles stood then to pour two drinks. He handed one to the doctor, who remained standing. The man took a sip of whiskey, then grimaced and looked at the amber liquid in his glass before lifting his eyes to Miles'. "I have reiterated to the Blairs that the lass requires complete rest and should not be moved. She should remain here under your care."

Miles looked toward the corridor. "She's not stirring then?"

"Not yet." The doctor sighed. "I expect that she will awaken once her body recovers from the shock."

The doctor finished his drink and left, stating he'd return the next morning and asked that he be notified if Siobhan woke before then. Miles remained in the front room until the Blairs came back from the bedchamber, and he stood to greet them.

Owen Blair stated, "I am sorry for this inconvenience."

"I have a second bedroom where I can sleep. There is no need for apologies," Miles replied. "If one of you wishes to remain here, I can sleep in one of the servants' rooms."

Both Zinnia and Amelia looked appalled at the mere thought of him, a titled gentleman, sleeping in servants' quarters. But then Zinnia appeared to reconsider her opinions.

"If I can take advantage of your hospitality, I would like to remain with my daughter for a bit longer," Siobhan's mother stated. "But then I will go home for the night and return tomorrow."

"Of course," Miles replied, then looked at Amelia. "You are welcome to remain as well."

She tossed her head and gave him a sour look.

So he turned to speak to Owen. "I can have my coachman take them home."

Owen looked from his wife to Amelia. "Will you stay with your mother?"

Amelia gave Miles a droll look. "I will return home with Papa. There is nothing I can do for my sister at the moment."

Once the two had left and Siobhan's mother returned to sit by her daughter, Miles joined her. Siobhan seemed to be asleep, her face soft, lips slightly parted.

Despite Zinnia Blair's usually haughty ways, right now she seemed genuinely upset. Miles felt badly for her, until she spoke. "I must make an appearance at the Frederickson's gala tomorrow night. It will not do for people to know something has happened to Siobhan. The gossips will have a field day."

"What happened to her was not her fault." Miles could not keep the anger from his tone.

The woman studied the sleeping lass for a moment. "It *is* her fault," she replied with hushed displeasure. "If only she kept from going to those dreadful places. I tried to warn her. It was not safe."

Miles could not help but agree. Still, Siobhan's desire to help the underprivileged family wasn't going to be deterred no matter how many warnings she received. "I understand her friend's brother usually accompanies them."

Zinnia blew out a breath. "Be that as it may. This time, she went alone. The coachman told us she told him to visit with family and they'd agreed she'd wait for him in the carriage if he hadn't returned. He'd expected to be back much sooner, he said, but was delayed because of an issue with his elderly mother. By the time he'd returned, she'd been taken. But he never should have left. He should have known better."

There was nothing more to be said. Of course, Siobhan hadn't demanded he stay with the carriage. She would be concerned that he attend to his family. But it was obvious her mother needed someone to blame to feel better about the situation and the driver was an easy target.

"Siobhan will remain here as long as the doctor thinks she should. When I am not here I will ensure Firtha, my housekeeper, remains vigilant."

It was getting dark when the woman finally went home, and the house grew silent. Miles ate his supper in silence, which didn't bother him. He was used to eating alone, often taking advantage of the moment to consider his schedule for the following day.

He, too, had been invited and had responded that he would attend the Frederickson's gala. But since Siobhan's mother hadn't indicated anyone would be at her daughter's bedside, Miles could not see leaving her alone, even if with his staff.

"My lord, will you require anything else tonight?" Firtha asked, her face serene. "I have prepared the spare bedchamber for you. All you will need tonight is there."

"Thank you. Go get some rest. I will not go to bed for a while. I plan to sit with our guest for a bit."

THE SILENCE OF the house was only broken by the night sounds outside: the occasional hoot of an owl, a carriage passing by, and every so often a tree branch hitting the side of the house.

Miles lowered to the chair next to Siobhan's bed with a book. He studied the sleeping beauty for a long moment, noting the rhythmic lifting and lowering of her chest and how the coloring was returning to her face.

Unable to stop himself, he reached over and lightly touched the side of her face. A bruise had formed on her jaw. There were reddened scratches on her wrist where she'd fought against the binds, and he lifted her hand to study them. Any other injuries he could not see but he was sure she was probably bruised in other places from the fall.

Her eyes fluttered, causing his breath to catch.

"Siobhan. Siobhan. Can you hear me?" He spoke in a low tone to keep from startling her. Miles slid his hand from just above her wrist to clutch her hand. "You are safe now. Here in my home."

Once again her eyes fluttered, but they didn't open. What if she never awakened? Was it possible she'd die in her sleep while no one was there to ensure she was not alone? Worry whirled around him like a magician's wand, swirling both fear and apprehension.

He brought her delicate hand to his mouth and pressed a kiss to the knuckles, allowing his lips to linger longer than appropriate, the feel of her skin settling his erratic emotions.

"Wake up. Look at me. I wish to see those beautiful blue eyes," he whispered into her ear. "I know you can hear me."

SOMETHING TOUCHED THE side of his face, and he opened his eyes to a beautiful scene. Flowers floated, scented pillowy clouds hung low to where he could reach out and touch them. Happy birdsong filled the air and Miles wanted to remain there forever.

Something about the atmosphere changed when the ground shifted, making him feel as if he plummeted from a great height.

"Miles?"

The soft voice permeated the air, and Miles jerked awake. He'd fallen asleep with his head on the bed next to Siobhan's shoulder. Blinking away the sleepiness, he stiffly sat up only to realize Siobhan was watching him with unconcealed curiosity. "Why am I here?"

"You're awake," he replied as a broad grin split his face. It was the first time in years he'd felt true happiness, and it filled him completely.

Her lips curved into a soft smile. "So are you." Then she

looked around the room. "Where are we?"

"This is my bedchamber. You had a bad fall yesterday. I brought you here." He wished to be more alert in order to explain things, so he stood and stretched. "Do you remember anything?"

She shook her head, and then yawned. "No not really. I remember going to Susan's. Did I fall there?"

As he wasn't sure how to approach things, Miles diverted the conversation. "Your mother should be here shortly. Also, the doctor. I will ask my housekeeper, Firtha, to come and attend to any needs you have. You must remain in bed. The doctor was very firm."

For a long moment Siobhan studied him. "Have you been here all night?"

He nodded. "By the way my back and neck protest, I am sure I have."

"Mother and Father know I am here?" She slid a glance to the doorway as if expecting them to enter. "No one remained here for the night?"

"I believe your father had business to attend to," Miles said, leaving out that her father was planning to speak to the constable again. Someone would no doubt arrive soon to get his statement and description of the assailant.

Siobhan sighed, her eyes closing for just a second. "Mother and Amelia are probably preoccupied with the gala tonight."

"Your mother assured me she will come to see about you first thing."

By the feeble light outside and lack of sounds in the house, Miles guessed it to be very early yet. "I will bring you some tea."

"You do not have to. It is too early to wake anyone yet. Please go rest. I can wait for a while longer."

It was probably best that he go and at least change out of the clothes he'd worn since the day before. Once the doctor, and especially, her mother arrived, his attire would be noticed.

"I will go refresh and change. In the meantime, do not try to get up." He leaned down and met her gaze. "Promise me to stay put."

Siobhan's eyes were already drooping, and she yawned. "I promise," she said softly.

There was little doubt that in a few minutes she would be sound asleep again.

Once in the spare bedroom, Miles allowed his body to sag with relief. Not only was Siobhan awake, but she seemed to have retained her normal personality. He'd been sick with worry that she would never wake and have to be taken to a sanitarium to be looked after until death. A chuckle escaped at recalling how wild his imagination had gotten in the dark hours of the night.

Now his chest was light, the heaviness gone. In the mirror's reflection, he looked no worse for the wear. In truth, his body was probably accustomed to the late nights in the gentlemen's club or from entertaining a woman or two.

After removing his clothes, Miles went about washing his body. Every thoughtful, Firtha had hung a pair of complete outfits for him to pick from. He chose a gray suit that was comfortable to wear when spending most of the day at home. He'd no plans to leave that day unless someone or something required his immediate attention. Instead, he'd stay with Siobhan. There was nowhere and no one with whom he'd rather be; he didn't allow himself to wonder why.

CHAPTER SEVEN

S IOBHAN COULD NOT believe she'd somehow ended up at Lord Miles' home. Surely, both her mother and Amelia were terrified she'd do something scandalous. As soon as her mother arrived, Siobhan expected to be lectured on how to carry herself and act around Miles.

She was sure they did not have anything to worry about; after all, the poor man had seen her at her worst. She guessed that her appearance was appalling, with her hair askew and from the throbbing pain, perhaps with a swollen and bruised jaw.

If anything, Lord Miles would keep his distance using the excuse of her illness.

When she tried to sit up, pain tore from the back of her head to her left side, and she could not stop from crying out.

Within moments, two men and a woman rushed into the room and surrounded the bed. Miles, an older man who she assumed was the butler, and a woman wearing an apron stared down at her with questioning looks.

"What happened?" Miles asked, moving closer and touching her hand. "Are you in pain?"

Siobhan sniffed and nodded slowly. "I tried to sit up and it hurt horribly. But I must…" she hesitated, and looked at the woman as her face heated. To even mention such a thing in front of Miles was beyond embarrassing.

"I will assist her, my lord," the woman stated. "I have looked after many a woman right after delivery. There is no need to fret, dear." She made shooing motions with both hands urging the men to leave. Then the woman's warm gaze met hers. "I am Firtha. Now lass, let us try to get you to relieve yourself without moving overmuch."

Indeed Firtha was well versed in assisting invalids because she knew exactly what she needed and how to get it done most efficiently. She only had to lift her hips as the woman saw to her needs. Although it was mortifying, the relief of pressure took any embarrassment away.

"I wish to sit up," Siobhan insisted.

"The doctor urged us to not allow it until he has examined you," Firtha told her. "But I can assist you to drink a bit of tea. I will return shortly."

Firtha was a godsend. Not only did she wash Siobhan's face, hands, and arms, but she managed to brush her hair to the side and braid it so that it wasn't tugging on her wound or uncomfortable to lie on. Although the back of her head was not touched, Siobhan knew she was much more presentable.

She'd just finished the last of the tea, which had been spooned into her mouth by Firtha, when the doctor entered the room.

Miles had yet to return, and she was nervous about seeing the doctor alone. "Can Lord Miles come in while you are here?" she asked in a trembling voice. She wasn't sure why the thought of Miles staying with her made her less fearful, and indeed, he probably had no desire to be in the room with her and the physician. Even though her hair was brushed, and her face was clean, she was fairly sure she still appeared frightful and nothing like the attractive young women that he no doubt preferred.

Still, the doctor nodded and walked out. Siobhan was surprised when he returned moments later with Miles. She was even more surprised to see Lord Miles looking at her with a huge smile on his face as well as concern in his eyes. "As I told you, my lord, the lass is a bit scared," the doctor said, pulling instruments from his bag.

Although Miles remained by the door, his presence was comforting. "You will be fine, Miss Blair. Do not fret."

"Where is Mother?" she asked. "She should be here by now."

Both men remained silent, not knowing the answer to her question. Of course her mother was a late riser, but she expected that because of the circumstances, she'd get up earlier to come and see about her.

Tears burned her eyes and Siobhan blinked them away. This was the most humiliating experience. Surely Miles felt as uncomfortable as she did.

The doctor was efficient, looking into her eyes and listening to her heart.

"My lord, I require your assistance to turn her to her side."

Siobhan closed her eyes, feeling shocked. Surely, this was not proper. Two men—one of them an eligible bachelor—were about to touch her very personally. It was necessary of course, but surely her mother should be there.

Before she could refuse, they made quick work of turning her onto her right side. Miles rested his hands on her left shoulder and waist while the doctor lifted. She opened her eyes, whimpering at the pain it caused and gasped in panting breaths until it lessoned.

The doctor must have motioned for Miles to turn away, because he gave her his back so the doctor could examine her shoulder and hip.

"Did you know that Doctor Ralston has been my doctor since I was a wee lad? He is our family physician," Miles said, obviously doing what he could to distract her. She concentrated on Miles' voice, doing her best to ignore the fact a strange man was touching her body, though his reason to do so was only to learn if it hurt, or if she was tender.

"Will you tell me what happened?" she asked no one in particular.

The doctor pushed back on her left shoulder, and she grunted. "That hurts."

"It may be displaced," the doctor replied, and she had no idea what that meant. "What do you remember?"

"I remember going to Susan's house. She is a widow I visit. I do not remember leaving. The next thing I knew I was waking up here."

The doctor let out a breath. "My lord. Please…?"

This time the men helped her onto her back and then, with his arms under hers, Miles slid her up to sit while the doctor placed pillows behind her back.

Siobhan was mortified that she began to cry at the pain the movement caused, but at the same time she was relieved not to be on her back. Within moments the pain became unbearable, and they had to reposition her so that her hips were flat. It was not as painful, but at least she could look around and see more than just the ceiling.

"Your hip is very bruised. Not broken," the doctor explained. "You should be able to sit longer in a day or two. For now, it is best you recline." He frowned. "If your parents do not arrive shortly, I will pay them a visit to inform them of your bettered condition. I am certain you will be out of bed and about within a matter of days."

Siobhan looked at Miles who listened with an unreadable expression. "Can I go home?"

"I would prefer you not be moved until the day after tomorrow at the earliest." The doctor turned to walk away.

"Doctor Ralston, you have yet to tell me what happened," Siobhan called out, stopping him.

"I will explain it to you," Miles said. "Doctor, I will walk you out."

He returned within moments and lowered into the chair next to the bed to begin recounting what he'd witnessed.

Siobhan strained to remember the incident. According to Miles, she'd been assaulted by two men and then one of them had tried to abscond with her. Closing her eyes, she did her best to recall the attack, but other than being at Susan's house, there were no further memories.

Firtha brought her a light breakfast, which she gobbled up.

Her stomach had felt empty all morning and she was grateful for the delicious food.

Just as she finished eating, her mother entered. "I had to see for myself that you are indeed awake." She neared and sat, not kissing, or touching her with any kind of reassuring gesture, which was her usual behavior. Still, Siobhan felt saddened. She was in so much pain and was so confused about what had happened, it would have been nice to have an affectionate gesture. Instead, her mother looked at Firtha, and said, "Be a dear and bring tea. Perhaps some biscuits if you have them."

Siobhan waited for whatever her mother would say next. In all probability it would be an excuse for not remaining long or returning that day. Of her parents, Siobhan preferred her father's company. Although somewhat distracted, he never shied away from expressing his affections. Her mother, on the other hand, was always distant. Although she had no doubts that her mother cared for her, it was obvious that Zinnia Blair was not the maternal kind of woman. And, too, she favored Amelia, though the reason for this escaped Siobhan. Maybe because her sister was easier to control and not as wont to do as she wished instead of what her mother expected a young woman to do.

"Darling," her mother began. "Doctor Ralston insists that you should not be moved. He informed me you cry out in pain when jostled."

"I wish to go home," Siobhan whispered. "It hurts, but I will withstand the pain not to continue this imposition on Lord Miles."

Her mother sat erect, her expression calculating. "Already I suspect people are aware there is something amiss."

"What do you mean, Mother?"

"For goodness sakes, you cannot be so naïve as to think you can remain in a bachelor's home overnight and that there be no repercussions."

"How can anyone possibly know I am here?" Siobhan's head swam and she had to put her hand out. "Please Mother, do not continue. My head is hurting."

Firtha walked in with a tray on which a teapot and cups were balanced as well as a small plate with iced biscuits.

"I will pour," her mother insisted.

"Miss Blair cannot sit up to drink the tea. She must be spoon-fed."

It was as if she'd informed her mother a snake was under the bed by the way she recoiled.

"I had breakfast. I do not require tea. Thank you, Firtha." Siobhan would have rolled her eyes if not for fear of a worse headache.

"As I was saying," her mother continued as she bit into a biscuit and sipped her tea. "It is most inappropriate for you to remain here in a single man's home with no chaperone in sight."

As usual, Zinnia worried more about what the gossips spewed than the fact her daughter was injured and had yet to attempt to walk.

"Mother, I am injured. His was the closest house. We have never been alone." She did consider that perhaps while Miles and she slept they'd indeed been alone, but it wasn't as if anything untoward occurred. She could not even sit up unaided; what could the gossips possibly think they were able to do?

"I brought you several night gowns and a robe. Also a hair-brush, a journal, and pencils. It will help time go by until you can come home," said her mother. Siobhan didn't bother pointing out that if she could not sit up to sip her tea, she was unlikely able to use a journal and pencils. As for the hairbrush, Firtha had managed to brush and braid her hair without requiring Siobhan to provide one from home. She was grateful for the nightgowns and robe, but hoped she would be away from Miles' house before she had need to use all of them.

Not fifteen minutes later, teapot empty and biscuits eaten, her mother stood. "I am glad to see you are better. However, I must get back. There is much to do before the Frederickson's gala tonight."

Siobhan's breathing hitched as she tried to formulate words, not wishing to sound like a spoiled child. "Mother, I wish to go home. Surely, we can manage it." She had to stop talking as her throat constricted. "P-please," she managed.

Her mother looked at the doorway as if more concerned about her escape than Siobhan's pain. "I would like to. But the doctor is adamant that you remain in bed without being moved in case your hip is splintered. He is very worried at the amount of discomfort you experience when you are moved."

"He said it was bruised, not splintered. And I can resist the pain," Siobhan replied, in spite of the determined look on her mother's face to not budge on the matter.

"We have more urgent matters to see about," she responded, and it was clear to Siobhan that her mother was already scheming ways to benefit from this situation.

Just then her father walked in and rushed to her. He leaned forward and pressed a kiss to each side of her face. With a wide smile, he peered down at her. "I am so thankful that you've awakened, darling one. It was a long night waiting to return to see about you."

"Owen," her mother said. "I was just informing Siobhan that because of the situation, action must be taken."

"I spoke to the constable. Someone will be here today to speak to Lord Miles and Siobhan. Although perhaps you cannot be much help since you cannot remember." He took her hand. "It is perfectly fine. Do not fret over much. I am sure the delinquent will be found and punished."

Siobhan squeezed her father's hand. "I agree. Surely plenty of people saw and someone will know him."

Her mother cleared her throat. "*That* is not what I was referring to."

Miles came to the door and regarded her with a warm look before acknowledging her parents. "Her countenance is better at your visit," he told them before he looked back at her. "You feel better?"

"I do," Siobhan replied.

"I am glad you are here," her mother said to Miles. "I am trying to inform Siobhan and my husband that action must be taken immediately to keep the gossips at bay."

All three looked at her with various expressions of confusion.

It was her father who finally spoke. "Zinnia, to what are you referring? I am growing grayer waiting for you to make your point."

Siobhan giggled but stopped when her mother's narrowed gaze snapped from her husband to her. "What I am stating is that Lord and Siobhan must marry immediately."

There was a stunned silence at her mother's comment.

"Marry?" Siobhan choked out. "Mother, Lord Miles has been gracious enough to allow me to be here. I've taken away his very own bedchamber. It is ridiculous that you give so much credence to the gossips as to even suggest such a thing."

Her mother turned to Miles. "It must be discussed. Obviously the fact that my daughter spent an entire night here without a chaperone is not to be taken lightly."

Mortified, Siobhan felt heat rise to her cheeks. Her mother was making the situation worse by the moment. "Mother, stop at once. This cannot continue."

Miles' expression was calm, except for the tightness of his jaw. "You can send a chaperone to remain here. I will go to my family residence to remove any reason for any gossip to spread."

Now Siobhan became enraged. "You will do no such thing. I will withstand the pain and be moved to my home at once. It is ridiculous that we cause you so much trouble after you were kind enough to save my life." Tears of frustration spilled down her cheeks.

"I am upsetting you," her mother stated, though it was obvious. "It is best I go for now. Unfortunately, you know I am right. Siobhan's reputation is now in tatters." Her mother patted Siobhan's hand, the only comfort she'd bothered to extend, and one Siobhan was sure she only performed for Miles' benefit. "My lord. You mentioned a spare room in the servant quarters. Can one of our maids stay for a few nights to see to Siobhan?"

"Of course," Miles said tightly.

Her father leaned over and pressed a kiss to her forehead. "Do not you worry. I am sure there will be no need for nuptials. Many times in history, situations like this were solved either by negotiation or in battle to a satisfactory ending."

Siobhan didn't bother trying to make sense of what her father was thinking. Instead she nodded and offered him a smile. "Thank you, Father."

"I will see you out," Miles said, giving her father a confused look. If not for the situation, Siobhan would have laughed at her father's peculiar attempt to make her feel better.

Her mother shook her head. "It must be marriage. Our daughter will be scorned by society, otherwise."

Miles motioned for them to go before him and followed them. In the corridor, they continued speaking about the spare room and accommodations for a maid.

Siobhan wanted to scream after them. Why wasn't Miles reacting more strongly? His voice was smooth and even, as if her mother had merely suggested that he and she go for a walk and not demanded marriage. In her mind, his courtesy toward her mother made the situation even worse and if she would have been able to walk, Siobhan would have dragged the woman from the house and demanded that she apologize to Miles.

She was not surprised when she was overcome by uncontrollable sobs that wracked through her body as waves of anger and frustration flowed over her. The fact that crying caused her so much pain made her sob harder and harder, until she could not breathe.

Miles re-entered the room and immediately came to her side. Because it was impossible for Siobhan to sit, he lay next to her and wrapped her in his muscular arms. With extreme care, he slid closer until they were flushed against one another.

Siobhan pushed her face into Miles' shoulder, soaking the

fabric of his waistcoat while grasping the fine, soft cloth.

"Shh," he whispered. "You must calm yourself or risk causing harm."

Siobhan did her best, taking deep breaths in between sobs, but it proved hard. Just when she began to gain control, another wave of sorrow would overtake her.

"Siobhan, what must I do to help you stop crying?" Miles asked, pressing his lips against her temple. "Must I tickle you? Kiss you?"

The words had the desired effect and she calmed to soft hitched breaths. "What?" She peered up at him. "What did you say?"

His lips curved. "I asked if I must kiss you."

Of their own accord her eyes moved to his lips, the very ones she'd often daydreamed of touching hers. "Why would you do that?"

His soft chuckled brought her to meet his hazel regard. "Perhaps because I have been thinking about it for a long time."

"That cannot be true." Siobhan let out a breath, sure that she looked every bit a mess. "Especially now. I must look like a troll."

"A beautiful troll," he jested.

Unable to say more, she let out a shaky breath. "I am so sorry…"

At once, Miles' lips covered hers and the world evaporated. The kiss was soft, gentle, but at the same time, passionate. Every part of her, mind, body, and soul united at that very moment sending tendrils of desire flowing through her.

Never before had she been kissed by a man in such a way with their bodies flush, and his strong arms around her in an intimate embrace and in bed, holding each other, their mouths exploring. His mouth traveled from her mouth to just below her ear. Tingles of awareness sent shivers down her spine. All thoughts of pain and discomfort disappeared, and warmth enveloped her in a blanket of overwhelming, wonderful sensations.

Miles deepened the kiss, suckling her lips, then trailed his lips from her mouth to her jaw, and when he kissed the side of her neck, Miles' tongue darted out, wet and moist as it trailed across her sensitive skin.

Threading her fingers through Miles' thick hair, she held him in place, silently demanding he continue. His breathing hitched when she exhaled into his ear, which emboldened her to press a kiss to the soft flesh.

"We cannot," Miles murmured, slowly pulling away. "I do not wish to hurt you."

For a moment it was hard to comprehend what he said. Still enraptured and floating on air, she slowly opened her eyes to meet his.

"Your eyes are dark," Miles said, with a warm smile. "I wondered if they would darken when you're kissed, like they do when you are annoyed."

Her cheeks warmed and with a trembling hand she pushed her hair back. Words escaped her. Exhaling, Siobhan met his gaze. "Goodness."

It was nice that he didn't move away but instead kept his arms around her, holding her in place. Siobhan wondered if perhaps her mother's demand had merit. The embrace brought peace and safety, a comfort of knowing she was protected. Truly, she could spend days in his arms.

"I ruined your waistcoat," she remarked, studying the damp and crumpled fabric. "I am so upset at Mother for not taking me home. I should not remain here. The last thing you need is her coming up with a plan to ensnare you into marriage."

"It will be worked out. I am an expert at avoiding unwanted attempts by overzealous mothers," he replied.

The statement almost made her cringe. Of course, the man had no desire to marry her. Besides, she herself wasn't interested in marriage to a man who'd been forced into marrying her.

Despite the affirmation, his statement still felt like a rejection.

Siobhan tried to push away, but his arms remained steadily

around her. "We should not remain like this. Someone could walk in. I am calmed, I promise." Unfortunately she spoiled her promise with a sniffle that confirmed she remained saddened.

"You are welcome to stay here as long as you wish," Miles stated, a crease forming between his brows as he seemed to realize what he'd said could have come across as rude. "Do not feel that I am bothered by your being here. As you can probably tell, I quite enjoy your company." He accentuated the words by pressing a kiss to the tip of her nose. "Understood?"

Siobhan nodded. "Did the doctor say anything else about what he thought caused so much pain when I move?"

"He thinks you bruised your left hip in the fall."

In his arms on her right side, Siobhan gingerly stretched her left leg, not realizing it caused her pelvis to thrust into Miles' leg until his eyes widened just a bit. The bruised area felt painful, but much less than it had earlier.

"I am so sorry," Siobhan said quickly heat infusing her face. "It does hurt, but it seems that if I lay on my right side, the pain is lessened."

"I will call Firtha to come see about you. I will be gone for a few hours. Rest, beautiful lass," he whispered and then he kissed her again.

The light press of his lips on hers lingered just a bit, and of their own volition, her eyes fell closed. He pulled away, and as she looked up at him, his lips curved. Carefully removing his arms from around her, he slid from the bed and stood. She could not drag her eyes from him. There had been bliss and a bit of passion, at least on her part. Although she had little idea what occurred between husband and wife, Siobhan was certain it would be as wonderful as being kissed by him.

Miles straightened his jacket and looked down at himself. "I best change before going out." He peered at her, a strange expression crossed his features momentarily. Then it was gone, making Siobhan wonder if perhaps it had been a figment of her imagination.

He left and it was as if she'd been holding her breath but was finally able to take in air fully. She inhaled and let out a long breath. Truly, having been in his arms was something she'd never, ever forget.

CHAPTER EIGHT

W HILE DRESSING, MILES kept replaying what had occurred with Siobhan. He'd meant to calm the lass, comfort her. The last thing he should have done was to have taken advantage of the situation.

He was a cad, there was no denying it, but had been never one to take unwelcome liberties. Although Siobhan had responded, her reaction did not excuse his actions. What had he done? Given her false hope of more between them?

He'd been disrespectful and had to apologize.

It was best to make things right immediately. He walked from the room and after a soft knock entered the larger bedroom where Siobhan was.

"I must apologize and beg for your forgiveness," he said, moving closer to the bed. "There is absolutely no excuse for the liberties I took. I will ensure it never happens again."

Siobhan searched his face for a long moment, her expression unreadable. "You do not have to apologize. It was a kiss, that is all it was."

It was his turn to study her. The way she readily made the statement, giving him leeway to not feel obligated in any way was quite surprising. Most women would have leaped on the opportunity to obtain something from him after less of an interaction. Whether money or marriage, there was always a catch every time he'd had any assignation with a woman. Better to ask and get the matter into the open as soon as possible so he could tend to it or eliminate it altogether.

"Do you require anything more from me?"

Siobhan shrugged, looking past him to a chair. "Can you assist me to sit there by the window? Please? I'm so tired of being in bed."

Miles turned to the chair in surprise. Then he almost laughed at the way he was acting, as if he didn't know there was a chair in his own room. "We can try, but if you are in any pain, back to bed you will go."

A mischievous twinkle in her eyes, she smiled. "If I can sit, then I will demand to go home. Let's try it."

"Very well," he replied, not convinced it was something he should do. Or even, wanted to do. But that was ridiculous; hadn't he just worried that she would demand marriage from him for a kiss? And still, he wanted her to stay in his home, unchaperoned. Her mother was not wrong in her own demands of marriage.

Just as he neared the bed and slid his arms under her arms and legs, there was a knock on the door. Miles froze as Firtha hurried inside. "My lord, what are you doing?"

"I asked to be moved to a chair," Siobhan replied with a breezy tone, as if discussing the weather.

"Absolutely not." The housekeeper neared and shooed him away. "Do not be fooled by a stunning beauty into doing things that are not recommended by the doctor, my lord. Her mother informed me she can be quite wily."

Siobhan scowled. It was her mother who schemed and laid traps. She was innocent of the trait. "I feel a bit better."

"And if you rest another day, you will feel even more so," Firtha replied while pulling the blankets back over Siobhan's legs and up to her waist.

Miles winked at Siobhan. "You have saved me from her cunning," he said to Firtha. He wondered if it was possible for the housekeeper to save his heart as well.

"HA!" GRANT SAID, lifting his glass. "The most eligible bachelor in Glasgow admits defeat." Miles had admitted that he'd not come up with the funding by other means and would instead pay from his own coffers. Much to the delight of his companions, who'd been convinced he'd win the wager; instead, they could now make fun of him.

Along with Henry and Evan, the four friends lounged at Henry's home. The room had been decorated in masculine tones with dark furniture and a sideboard with decanters of whiskey, brandy, and a variety of other libations. There were comfortable chairs with tables strategically placed to allow for setting down one's glass and an enormous plush rug to cushion their feet. They'd be there for about an hour, discussing the ship's departure and the expectation of what they'd do upon its return.

Evan would be in charge of selling the precious cargo, as he worked for his family's textile company. Astute with money from helping manage their families' fortune, Henry and Miles would assist with investments. Lastly, the best of them in the art of travel and entertainment, Grant was to plan a trip abroad for the men and their wives.

"I am not sure to go on the trip," Miles stated, and then waited for their reaction. It was not surprising to note his statement was met with scowls of disapproval.

Henry was first to respond. "Of course, you will travel with us. This venture was started by the four of us and the four of us will finish it."

"You will all be traveling with your wives and—" he looked at Evan—"children."

"That is not of importance," Evan stated. "We all know you will probably never marry. You are our children's honorary uncle. You are our family."

Miles pretended to wipe a non-existent tear. "I am deeply

touched."

"Find someone, invite the woman along. You may find it to be a delight." Grant, who'd rarely been without female companionship before marrying the lovely Wren, was quick to give advice.

It surprised him that the only woman who came to mind when considering a travel companion was Siobhan. A clear picture of the beautiful lass beside him on a ship was indeed enticing.

"He is smiling," Henry informed the others. "Look at his face, I do believe he is considering it."

Grant laughed, meeting Miles' eyes. "There *is* someone." He pointed at Miles. "His expression proves it in spite of his denial."

The other three leaned forward to look at him closely as if they'd be able to discern who he was thinking about. Miles did his best not to squirm, stretching his legs out and assuming a look of boredom, his signature way of deflecting any speculation. His friends were not fooled for one instant. They'd known each other since they were lads and probably recognized his tells.

Evan gave a slight nod and leaned back in his chair. "If you do not tell us, we shall investigate."

Just as he was about to deny the existence of any woman, three beauties burst into the room. The ringleader, Felicity, who was Evan's wife and Grant's sister, came to stand in front of Miles. The other two flanking her were Hannah, Henry's wife, and Wren, Grant's wife.

"The talk is all over town," Felicity stated, her eyes bright with excitement. "Is it true? Siobhan Blair is currently staying at your townhouse after you heroically rescued her from a horrible man who tried to kidnap her." She took a breath. "Tell us everything! There is talk of marriage as she remained at your home *unchaperoned*."

The entire group's eyes focused on Miles. The three men's faces held grins, as if they knew more than the women did.

Miles opened his mouth and hesitated, surprised by their

curiosity, and even more so, surprised by his lack of dismay. Instead, he could feel his heart warming and expanding at the thought of Siobhan. The noose was tightening, but his desire to avoid it was not. "I… there is not to be any marriage. The…lass is injured, and the doctor recommended she is not to be moved. Someone has been there…" He shrugged, not finishing the statement. If he said anymore, he knew his friends would use it to tease him.

Besides, and more importantly, he knew Siobhan would be mortified upon learning that she was the subject of gossip. Her mother had not been lying or exaggerating.

"If you do not marry her, she will be ruined," Hannah stated in her usual soft voice. "She is from a family that is highly regarded among your peers." She motioned to the men in the room. Hannah was from a working-class family, and, for that matter, so were Grant and Felicity. However, their father had accumulated quite a fortune as actuary for the wealthiest families in Glasgow.

Henry chuckled. "We should have wagered on it. It appears that our friend, the esteemed and desirable Lord Miles, has finally been ensnared in a trap." The other men laughed, while the women looked on in disapproval.

"It is not funny," Felicity informed them with a stop of her foot. "The poor lass. Injured and fueling the grist for the gossips."

Miles let out a breath. "If there are rumors all over town, it is because her mother is spreading them. She immediately insisted that there had to be a marriage as I brought the lass to my house after she fell from a horse and was rendered unconscious."

"Why to your house?" Grant asked. "You could have taken her to her home."

Ire rose, not only at his friends' inquisitions but by the fact that now the rumors would need to be squashed, especially for Siobhan's sake. "Because it was the closest. You do not understand. She was unconscious and barely breathing."

"Of course," Felicity said patting his shoulder. "You did what you thought best to save her life. You are a hero."

Felicity's words filled him with conflicting emotions. "I am no such thing," he replied, trying to sound nonchalant. Then he stood. This could not be allowed to continue. "I must go see about this situation." He nodded at the women and proceeded to the doorway. Henry followed him.

As a member of one of the wealthiest families in the city, Henry was well aware of the conniving mothers who all but threw their daughters in front of a wealthy, and especially a titled, bachelor. "What are you going to do?" His friend's blue gaze met his. "Do not make the situation worse. I propose you move into your parents' home immediately until the rumors die down. Ensure your mother's acquaintances see you there. That way they will—hopefully—quell any talk of you and the lass being alone and unchaperoned."

The idea had merit. Miles shook his head in annoyance at how much society dictated their lives. "I will do that. I am sure Mother will have advice and help me find a way out of this mess."

"Are you sure not to care for the lass? What is her name? Siobhan, is it?" Miles paused as Henry asked. "Because if you do, what Hannah said is true. She may be ruined. You know how shallow our peers are."

Miles didn't want to think about it. He'd never planned to get married, and had worked hard never to get trapped into the institution. The irony that he was responsible for placing himself in this position where he'd have to marry Siobhan to save her reputation wasn't lost on him. "I'd best go," Miles said, accepting Henry's reassuring pats on his shoulder.

WHEN HE ARRIVED at his townhouse, his stomach fell at seeing a familiar carriage already there. The Miles' crest told him it was either his mother, father, or even his entire family there.

Without waiting for his own carriage to come to a full stop, he threw open the door and jumped down, hurrying to the front door. His butler, Jones, opened it, giving him a sly look.

"Your mother and sister are in your chambers with our guest."

Miles stopped himself from cursing aloud. "What happened?"

"They arrived asking if the rumors were true." Jones gave him a helpless shrug. "I told them you and the miss were never alone."

"Thank you, Jones." He handed the man his overcoat and hurried up to his bedchamber, taking the stairs two at a time. Before entering, he hesitated at the sound of laughter—his sister's giggles accompanied by his mother's more reserved chuckles—from inside. It was a good sign, he supposed; it was good that the women appeared to be getting along and were enjoying each other's company, but at the same time, he realized it was going to make it harder to deny their probable expectation that he would marry Siobhan. He prepared himself for the inevitable battle by squaring his shoulders and straightening the hem of his jacket, before walking into the room. Their three faces turned to the door at his arrival, all of them bright and smiling. "Good evening, Mother, Sister. I did not expect you to be here."

"That is obvious." His mother's expression became serious. "Why did I have to hear from the gossips that my son is embroiled in a scandal?"

She accepted his kisses to her cheeks, then slid a look at Siobhan. "The poor lass has been telling us what occurred."

"It is rather amusing," Penelope added, with a broad grin. "You have to admit it."

"You found it comical?" Miles asked, looking at Siobhan who watched his interaction with his mother with an expression of fascination that he found hard to fathom.

His mother shook her head. "It is not the situation that is funny. Of course not. But the lass has a way of telling things in quite an animated fashion."

Of course, Siobhan would ensure that his mother and sister were immediately aware there was nothing to worry about, and especially, that the rumors about them were untrue. However, he found it troubling that no one from her family was currently present as well.

"Has anyone from your family come to see you?" he asked.

Siobhan replied with a one-shouldered shrug. "Mother and Amelia are probably recuperating after last night's ball. Father has a lecture to attend this afternoon." She looked at his mother. "I am hopeful they will fetch me to go home tomorrow first thing, Your Grace."

His mother nodded and patted Siobhan's hand.

"How are you feeling?" he asked, unable to tear his eyes from the beauty. Her hair was brushed, but down around her shoulders, and he realized that other than her most intimate acquaintances, no one would see her so casually coiffed. Seeing her sitting up with pillows behind her and in his bed, with her hair tumbling down over her figure like a cape, sent all types of unsuitable images through his mind.

Those images multiplied when her gaze traveled from his eyes to his mouth and back up. "So much better. The pain is bearable," she replied with a soft smile that was innocent, yet unbearably seductive. His body began to react in a manner inappropriate to the situation in more ways than one.

His mother, more perceptive than he wanted to admit, cleared her throat. "Penelope has offered to braid Siobhan's hair. Why do we not go to the sitting room? I wish to speak to you."

"Of course," he replied, realizing he'd yet to look away from Siobhan. He wanted to memorize the picture before him. To keep in his mind how the beauty who lay in his bed looked, from her expression to the way her hands currently clutched the blankets. If only they were clutching his hair, his shoulders…

"Miles?" His mother's voice penetrated his thoughts, and he turned to the door, motioning for her to go before him.

Once in the sitting room, she gave him a bright look. "Finally."

"What?" Miles waited for her to sit before he lowered himself next to her.

His mother frowned, and she clutched both hands against her chest. "Explain why you have the girl here without a chaperone. It is most inappropriate, Miles, you must realize that."

"What I find inappropriate is that her family makes absolutely no effort to be here. They offered to send a maid, but one has yet to arrive. She is alone most of the time."

His mother studied him for a long moment, stopping only when Firtha entered. "May I bring you something, Your Grace?" she asked, eyeing them both.

"Firtha, what do you think?" his mother asked, as she turned her attention to his housekeeper. "About the situation with the lass staying here without a chaperone?"

The housekeeper slid a look at Miles. "The lass was in a very poor state. From what I've seen, she would not have been able to go farther. Bringing her here was my lord's only option. Someone of her family should have remained." The housekeeper *tsked*. "If I may be so bold, Your Grace, her mother is not attentive in the least."

"That I gather," his mother stated. "Something must be done." She looked at the housekeeper. "Thank you, Firtha. You may go. I do not require anything at the moment."

When the housekeeper left, Miles poured brandy for himself and a ratafia for his mother. As he handed it to her, he asked, "Mother, what did you hear and from whom?"

"One of the ladies from my sewing circle informed me of what occurred. The rumors spread at the McIntyre's ball last night. I wasn't aware of course, because no one dared repeat gossip about my own son to me." She let out a breath. "Since you seem infatuated with the lass, perhaps it is best that you get engaged immediately."

Every part of him rebelled at her assertion. Well...almost every part of him. But his heart rebelled at his rebellion. *Inconceiv-*

able. He was suffering from attraction, and nothing more. "I am not infatuated and will not be forced into marriage by gossips."

His mother's eyebrows rose. "You struggled to drag your eyes from her."

"She is a beauty, I will admit. And I can't deny that seeing her in my bed was fetching."

"Miles!" His mother exclaimed, then giggled. "I do not want to know what you were thinking."

He drank from the glass and studied it; he didn't want to dwell on his thoughts—or his mother's—at this moment either. Finally, however, he was able to look at her. "I believe her family's absence is a part of her mother's way to ensure a marriage contract. First, she tried to get me to marry Siobhan's sister with a failed attempt in the garden. Now this."

"Do you think she arranged the kidnapping?" His mother's eyes rounded. "Oh my."

Miles waved her concerns away. "No, I do not think she would go so far, but she is definitely taking advantage of this situation. The rumors began because of her. No one else besides her—and the servants—knew Siobhan was here. My servants, however, are loyal to me and besides, who would listen to what news they share?"

His mother gestured excitedly. "You must speak to your father immediately. The lass is delightful, and in spite of my original misgivings, I do, in fact, believe she will be a good match. Some say she has too much spirit, and it's true that I originally believed that to be true. But now that I've had an opportunity to speak with her and see the two of you together, it is clear to me that you need a wife like her, one who is somewhat..." she paused, considering, before she finished, "*Lively.* There is no doubt she is from a respectable family, although, I would wish for a better suited mother-in-law for you."

Miles opened his mouth to disagree, but then she interrupted him. Clearly she'd made up her mind and would brook no argument from him. "Go home now, and send Gilda back to come stay with the lass. Your sister and I will remain here for a bit."

She dismissed him then and he had no choice but to do her bidding, unless he wanted to get into an argument with her that he knew beyond a doubt he would not win. Besides, by the time Miles climbed into the carriage, his temples had begun to pound, and lights were starting to swim before his eyes. He had neglected his self-care and allowed himself to become overwhelmed with stress. One of his headaches was coming on. "Oh no." He leaned sideways, closing his eyes, dreading what was to come and knowing there was no way to stop it.

CHAPTER NINE

S IOBHAN HAD TO admit she'd never thought to be so comfortable around the Duchess of Spencer and Miles' younger sister.

A small table had been relocated from the corner of Miles' bedchamber so that two chairs could be added. The duchess insisted that she and Penelope would join Siobhan for dinner.

"Have they discovered who attacked you?" Penelope asked, her hazel eyes so much like her brother's.

Siobhan shook her head. "I do not believe so. A constable came to get a description from Mi—I mean, his lordship. I do not remember anything past leaving the building in search of the coachman."

"I am sure they will find the horrible man," Penelope said with a firm nod.

The duchess met her gaze. "Are you aware that you are the talk of society? By now, everyone is aware that you've spent two nights here without a chaperone."

Siobhan knew her face was red by the heat that crept up from her neck. "I am so very sorry. Mother was supposed to send someone. I begged to be taken home as soon as I awoke, to avoid any talk."

"There is no need for you to apologize," the duchess insisted. "Your mother should have known better than to leave you here this way, unchaperoned."

It was best to be completely honest, so Siobhan forged ahead. "Mother is trying to trap Mi—his lordship—into marriage. Rest assured, Your Grace, I will not allow it."

"Your reputation will be ruined," Penelope protested. "Your prospects for a good marriage gone."

Siobhan was glad when Firtha entered with tea, making it unnecessary for her to reply. And, it was true, she was especially glad the housekeeper had included a tincture as her pain had returned and was getting stronger as the day had passed. Taking the cup, she drank down the contents. "Thank you so much."

"You are in pain, and here we are, worrying you." The duchess looked at her daughter. "We should go and allow you to rest."

"Before you go, Your Grace," Siobhan interrupted, "Please realize how sincere I am in stating that I will not force his lordship to marry me. As I have informed your son, if I never marry, I will be content to spend my days helping my father with his historical research."

The duchess chuckled. "I am sure things will be worked out, and I doubt seriously that you will remain unmarried."

AFTER THE DUCHESS and Penelope left, Siobhan could barely keep her eyes open. Before she fell asleep, a woman named Gilda arrived, though she wasn't sure if she'd been sent by her mother or procured by orders of the duchess. Either way, she had plans to remain until it was time for Siobhan to go home.

"Who sent you?" she asked.

"Her grace," Gilda replied. Siobhan could not believe her mother had not sent someone as yet. This was most embarrassing. Yet her mother would not see it that way, and it became more and more obvious that her current plan was to spread rumors to ensure one of her daughters married a title.

She woke up later in the day. Gilda assured her that Miles had not returned to see about her, so she assumed he'd gone out. Strange that she'd become accustomed to seeing him regularly.

Disappointment filled her when he did not appear the following morning or afternoon.

The doctor came and proclaimed that her bruised hip was healing astonishingly fast. Again, she wondered why Miles was not there to speak to the doctor. Not even outside of the bedroom; she listened, straining to hear his voice, but all she heard was the doctor bidding the butler good day, and the door opening and closing for him to leave.

It was late afternoon before her mother and Amelia finally arrived.

"The doctor came to inform us that we can take you home now." Her mother looked around the room. "Have you seen his lordship today?"

"I have not seen him since yesterday," Siobhan said, making sure she used a neutral tone that didn't display her disappointment. "I am sure he has better things to do than to keep me company."

Her mother pressed her lips together. Unlike Siobhan, she made no effort to hide her emotions. "So he has not been here at all?"

"I do not believe so. Especially after the rumors started." She fixed her mother with as stern a stare as she could muster. "I am sure he went to stay at his family estate."

"Most rude, to leave a guest alone." Her mother stalked to the window to peer out. "Where is your father with the larger carriage?"

"Why did you come separately?" Siobhan asked, expecting that her mother wished to ensure she had enough room to lay comfortably in the larger coach.

Instead her mother gave her a prim look. "Your sister and I have an appointment with the seamstress that I could not possibly cancel. You are aware how hard it is to be seen by Madam LeVeon, now that she's gained popularity."

Although she should have been used to it by now, her mother's focus on herself and her own interests—and those of her sister—and her lack of caring for Siobhan stung deeply.

Tears gathered in her eyes and Siobhan blinked them away. "Will you ride to the house with me, at least? It will be painful."

Her mother seemed stunned at the request. "Do you really think so? You seem so much better than the last time I visited."

As much as she tried to hold them in, a few tears spilled down her cheeks. She swallowed away the lump in her throat and tried to appear unaffected. "I am in horrible pain even now, Mother. Every movement hurts."

When her mother and sister exchanged looks that seemed to commiserate how annoying they thought her protests, Siobhan looked away. "Never mind. I am sure Papa will see after me." Her voice cracked.

"You must understand. If we could cancel the appointment, we would." Amelia's tone was less than believable.

"Of course," Siobhan said.

The sound of the front door could be heard, and the deep timbre of male voices.

"Here he is," her mother announced with obvious relief, at hearing her husband. When he arrived in the doorway, she told him, "Owen, bring the coachman. She will have to be carried out."

As her mother and Amelia looked on, Miles' butler, the family coachman, and her father lifted her from the bed. Siobhan did her best to keep from crying out in pain, but in the end, she gave up and whimpered.

It was a cumbersome affair to get her through the doorway, down the corridor and outside to the coach. By the time she was settled inside the coach, tears poured freely down her face. Siobhan knew it was not only from pain, but because she knew Miles had purposely stayed away. Not that she could blame him, but it was hard to explain that to her wounded heart.

Through the carriage door, her father was thanking the butler and handing him a note. Probably for Miles, to thank him. Of all the people in her family, only her father was conscientious enough to do such a thing.

As expected, the drive home was uncomfortable. Thankfully, the tincture Firtha had given her before the men carried her out to the carriage began to take effect, and she fell asleep halfway there.

As EXPECTED, BEING moved into the house and bedroom was uncomfortable, but Siobhan was prepared for it. Thankfully, she was able to sit with minor discomfort and she convinced her father to allow her to sit by the window. Through the window Siobhan watched over the garden, the birds flying from one branch of a tree to another, and the butterflies fluttering over open blossoms, their graceful flights across brightly colored petals lulling her to relax.

Her mind went to the time she'd stood on a balcony talking with Miles. The way he spoke, his deep voice filling her senses. The way he'd understood her desire to get away from the crowds. A long sigh escaped her, as a smile played on her lips.

How long before she saw him again? She could not help but wonder, even though she knew that, because of the rumors, he would probably keep his distance.

Knocks on the door brought her out of her musings. Her father entered, his eyes bright with excitement.

"I met a young man named Charles Winthrop at the Historian's meeting. He told me he'd recently met you and that you'd invited him to meet with me. So he returned with me after the meeting. He ate dinner with me, your mother and your sister. But he stayed even after they'd retired, and we stayed up until late as he described his travels."

Siobhan smiled at her father's enthusiasm. No longer traveling as much as he'd once done, now he enjoyed learning from anyone who traveled recently.

"I knew you and he would have much to discuss." She held her breath to hear about what had occurred.

Happy about the discussions with the younger man, her sweet father lowered himself into a chair, grinning. "Yes. Charles regaled us with tales of his travels. Amelia was quite impressed, and accepted his invitation for a turn in the garden." He chuckled. "I admit to having cut their time short, wishing to spend more time learning of the historical locations and what new knowledge and artifacts are available."

Relief came over her. Perhaps if her mother was distracted with making a match for Amelia, she'd forget about Miles.

"It all sounds wonderful, Father. I am so glad I suggested he contact you."

"Yes! Well on you!" Her father exclaimed, and she could not help but smile at him. Although she didn't share an enthusiasm for history to the depth he did, she had always enjoyed their talks and helping him with his research. Through his love of historical studies, they'd found a bond, which meant that Siobhan was very well-versed on the subject, by default.

"Can you help me to stand?" Siobhan asked. "I must begin walking in order to heal faster." She knew she was acting without permission from the doctor, but in her mind it was best to rehabilitate herself and loosen up her stiff muscles without too many witnesses to see how painful it was to walk. The last thing she wanted was to fail and have Amelia looming triumphantly over her.

"Of course, yes." Her father stood and helped her to stand. To her shock, there was minimal pain. As a matter of fact, standing seemed more of a relief than sitting on her bruised hip.

With her father hovering close, she took a tentative step and then another. With each step, she relaxed more and more until she declared, "It doesn't hurt. Well, not as much as I expected." She smiled up at her father. "I am so relieved I could cry."

"This is wonderful, Siobhan. You may be able to attend to-morrow when we visit the Johnstones," her father stated, holding his hands out in case she required assistance. "Your mother and I have sent a message to let them know we will arrive at mid-day, and they replied with a welcome."

At the statement, Siobhan's heart stopped, and she gasped. She knew her eyes were wide as she looked up at her father, whose expression had turned serious.

"What is it? Are you in pain?"

"Father," Siobhan spoke as slowly as she could despite her thundering heart. "Why are we going to the Johnstone's?"

"To discuss the terms of your engagement to Lord Miles. Your mother told me she'd informed you of the need for this, as the rumors are rampant." He waved a hand dismissively. "I myself have not heard anything, but then again, the historical group has better things to speak about."

Siobhan grabbed his arm. "I cannot force Lord Miles to marry me! He will hate me forever."

Her father patted her hand. "He is an honorable young man. I quite like Miles Johnstone. His temperament and yours are compatible. As I told my friend Rufus once…"

Siobhan stopped listening, allowing him to guide her back to the chair as he rattled on about the history of arranged marriages and how they seemed to end up as better marriages than those created by love and passion.

"I will go tomorrow," she interrupted him. "Promise me that I can go, no matter what Mother says. It is my life, after all."

"I do not see why not," her father said, giving her another absent pat, this time on her head. "You know, this has given me an idea for a lecture for the Historians. I think I'll go do some more research." He left, mumbling about perhaps organizing a talk on arranged marriages.

BOTH HER MOTHER and Amelia were surprised when they walked

in later that day to find Siobhan at the dinner table. Despite a bit of discomfort, she wanted to appear to be healthy enough to go to the Johnstones' the following day.

Once there, she'd seek out Miles and together they could find a way out of what her mother had concocted. There was a chance the duke and duchess already had a plan to keep their son from marrying her. Perhaps it included having him engaged to someone of their choosing.

She frowned at the sinking feeling that formed in her stomach at the thought of Miles with another woman.

"It seems being home has done wonders for your recuperation," her mother stated. "This is good. You will be able to go with us tomorrow."

"Father informed me," Siobhan said, not elaborating. If she appeared against the idea, there was a chance her mother would insist she stay behind.

"Yes, it is for the best to get you two engaged and put all the rumors to rest." Her mother studied Siobhan for her reaction with assessing eyes. "Do you agree?"

Siobhan nodded. "It is time to stop the rumors. I will never understand gossips, using their wicked tongues in ways that hurt people."

At her comment, her mother blinked rapidly, which showed Siobhan she was doing her best to hide that she was offended by the statement. "Did your father tell you how that wonderful young man Charles Winthrop was here?"

At the mention of Winthrop's name, Amelia became animated, her cheeks pinkening. Siobhan smiled. Although she and Amelia were very different and even though they weren't close because her sister regarded her as a rival, Siobhan was glad to see her happy.

"Amelia, do you have plans to see Mister Winthrop again?"

"He will be calling on me this afternoon," Amelia replied, sliding a look at her mother. "You must return from the Johnstones' straight away."

Through the rest of the meal, the next day was discussed until her father interrupted to inform them of his plans for the next research project on arranged marriages.

They'd all become accustomed to his sharing historical studies, and for once his excitement about his latest topic of great interest to all three of the women, though, Siobhan mused, for different reasons.

As she lay in bed later that night, Siobhan's mind was awhirl as she pondered how to get a private moment with Miles. Wavering between asking to speak to him and waiting to see if his family had a prepared excuse, she remained awake until late into the night.

THE NEXT AFTERNOON, Siobhan watched through the carriage window to see large trees passing by as they made their way down the winding road onto the Johnstone estate. They went by thick, neatly trimmed hedges and onto a widened area that allowed for several carriages to pass at once.

She'd only been to the estate once before, when the duke and duchess had held a huge spring ball. Siobhan had been awed by the wonder of the majestic home with its enormous columned entrance and extravagant marbled floors. It had been the event of the season that year and she'd never forgotten the splendor of it all. Every elite family in society had attended yet in spite of all the people, the massive ballroom had never felt crowded. This time, however, her nerves barely let her appreciate the views of the front lawn with its pond in which swans circled gracefully.

They were assisted from the carriage by uniformed footmen and greeted at the door by an austere butler who spoke in an even tone. "His Grace and Her Grace are expecting you in the parlor. Come with me." He motioned with his right hand before turning and walking away; they followed.

Interesting that the man had not mentioned Miles being present, but Siobhan figured there was no need to mention it, as obviously, he would be in attendance.

She'd never been in a private, family room at the Johnstone estate. In spite of the fact, it wasn't a public room, it was still extravagant in its décor. The room was circular with windows making up an entire wall. Thick, rich plum-colored draperies with golden embroidered edges hung from each window's dizzying height to puddle onto the marble floor. Through the windows, a lush flower garden was visible, and Siobhan stared at it a moment, wishing she were out there instead of in here. Her throat dry, she finally looked at the Duke and Duchess of Spencer.

The duke, Leon Archibald Miles, was a tall, handsome man. His dark skin was smooth and unwrinkled, making him seem as young as Miles. He had dark brown eyes and full lips. His gaze, however, was flat, making it hard to know what he thought.

By contrast, the Duchess Arabella Johnstone smiled warmly, her bright hazel eyes meeting hers. Breathtakingly beautiful, tall, and slender, she had blond hair that was pulled up into an intricate and flattering style.

Seen together, Miles' parents made a stunning couple; it was no wonder both Miles and his sister Penelope were good-looking as well. Unfortunately, neither of them were present, which bothered Siobhan. Why wasn't Miles here, as their parents discussed their future?

Not only that, but the fact that he was not there would make it impossible to find a way to speak to him privately. She hoped he was only delayed, and that he would be attending their visit shortly.

Once the greetings were complete, everyone sat. Tea and cakes were brought and although Siobhan could not bear the thought of eating, she sipped the tea to calm her nerves. They exchanged pleasantries, her mother extolling the beauty of their home, while her father interjected historical facts about the estate and the architecture of their house.

Finally, the duchess looked at Siobhan. "I am happy to see you up and about. How do you feel?"

"I am much better, thank you for asking, Your Grace." Siobhan's voice sounded hoarse to her own ears, and she took another sip of tea to moisten her dry throat.

"That is wonderful," the duchess replied, and turned to her parents. "And so...we must discuss the results of my son's decision to take this lovely girl to his townhouse to recuperate."

That the duke allowed his wife to begin the discussion about the matter at hand made it obvious that he was going to defer decisions about the current situation to his wife. Siobhan's stomach fell and her heart began thundering as she searched the room and the doorways in hopes that Miles would appear. There had to be a way to save him from being forced to marry her.

"I apologize for my son's absence," the duke stated, as if realizing she sought Miles' presence. "He is away for a couple of days."

Where could Miles possibly go during such a time? Siobhan frowned. Unless, of course, he'd gone somewhere as a way for him to get out of marrying her.

"Where did he go?" Siobhan asked.

"England," the duchess replied quickly. "Only for a few days."

Her mother gave her a pointed look, silently telling her to be quiet. "As I have stated, because society is aware of what occurred, I must insist they become engaged immediately."

Siobhan held her breath, waiting for one of Miles' parents to respond.

"We strongly agree," the duchess replied. "Once Miles returns, we shall host a gala to announce the engagement."

"What?" Siobhan blurted, a bit too loudly. Before her mother could stop her, she continued, "You cannot force him into marriage. He will hate me."

The duchess gave her a knowing look. "Miles will not hate you, dear. In fact, I believe him to be quite fond of you." Siobhan sat back, her mind awhirl.

"Siobhan, remain quiet, and allow us to discuss the particulars." Her mother's eyes danced with excitement, probably at knowing they'd be connected to such a family through the marriage.

"May I ask," her father interjected, speaking to the duke. "I hear you have a vast collection of ancient artifacts. Is it true?"

Her mother gave her husband a disbelieving look. "Owen, this is not the time for such things."

"I believe it is best to leave all the particulars of how to get our son and your daughter married up to you and my wife." The duke seemed relieved to be able to get away and stood, motioning to the door. "I do indeed have a collection, although I would not call it vast."

The men left the room, almost sprinting to the door, as if afraid their wives would stop them.

Siobhan stared agog at the closing door, wondering if she was dreaming. No one seemed to be taking the situation seriously. Or the fact that two people—their children!—were being forced to marry just because of stupid rumors.

Although, to her shame, in truth it was only Miles who was being forced. She knew she would gladly marry him, especially after their shared time in bed. At the thought, her cheeks went hot, and she quickly looked at their mothers, wondering if they noticed.

The women went into a discussion of color themes, and who would be invited. The duchess called for a maid to bring paper and quills so they could write things down. It was as if they'd forgotten she and Amelia were present. Or that it was Siobhan's wedding and that she would be the bride. Shouldn't they be asking her what *she* wanted? And what about Miles? What did he want?

"A dress," her mother exclaimed. "Siobhan, we must make an appointment with the modiste immediately."

"Lavender would be lovely on you," the duchess added.

"Your eyes are the most astonishing color. They seem to go from pale to dark blue, into a shade that seems almost lavender."

Siobhan tried to smile but failed. It was important to her that he be involved. This wasn't right, at all. "Have you discussed any of this with Miles?"

Something flickered in the duchess' expression and for a split second, she glanced toward the ceiling. "Yes, and he understands."

In that moment, Siobhan knew he was not gone, but was there, somewhere, on the estate. Had he purposely refused to be present? Was he so enraged that they'd banned him from being there?

Siobhan worried and listened as the mothers began making a guest list. "May I go sit in the garden? I require a bit of air."

"Of course, dear," the duchess said, then looked at her mother.

There was a slight hesitation on her mother's part. "You should be present for this. There is much to discuss, and we cannot linger."

"I will only be a moment," Siobhan explained, looking past the window to the flowers that swayed in the breeze. "The garden looks so lovely, I just want to see it."

"Very well," her mother finally acquiesced. "Make haste."

She moved as quickly as her bruised body allowed her, choosing to ignore the protests from her injured hip. Once outside the door, she motioned to a maid who arranged flowers in a vase. "Where is Lord Miles?"

The maid glanced at the stairwell, and it was clear that she wanted to let Siobhan know the truth in spite of what the duke and duchess had ordered. She spoke slowly and loudly in case they were overheard, but as she spoke she nodded her head and pointed with her chin at the stairwell. "He is gone for a few days."

"I understand," Siobhan told her. "Please...Is there a powder room upstairs, perhaps?"

It was obvious the maid understood what she was asking, and

she gave Siobhan a knowing look. "There is indeed a powder room on the third door on the right."

"Thank you," Siobhan whispered and hurried up the stairs.

Upon coming to the door, she lost her nerve and almost turned back. She knocked lightly, but there was no response. She glanced around to ensure no one was about, then rapped on the door a bit more loudly. "Miles?"

There was no reply, so she tried the doorknob. To her surprise, the door opened easily, and she slipped inside. After closing the door softly, she turned around to survey the room, but what she saw made her freeze.

The bed was disheveled, blankets half on and half hanging onto the floor. A strange moaning came from the other side, and she tiptoed to peer over the edge of the mattress where she was shocked to see Miles, wearing only a nightshirt, lying on the floor in the corner of the room. He seemed oblivious to her presence. Was he asleep?

Or worse, was he inebriated to the point of being passed out?

Her footsteps must have woken him because he mumbled something incoherent. Siobhan moved closer.

"Water. More drops," he rasped hoarsely, holding out a hand. But both his eyes were squeezed shut and he appeared to be in pain.

Siobhan spotted a pitcher on the table next to the bed and hurried to it. It held water; beside it was a glass and a small bottle with a stopper. She opened it and sniffed; it smelled medicinal, similar to the tincture the doctor had given her for her pain. Hoping it was what he needed, she poured water into the glass and then squeezed several drops of what she'd assumed was medication into it. Then she moved around the bed to him, leaning down to press the glass into his hand and helping him to wrap his fingers around it.

He drank greedily, finishing the water with great gulps, then held out the glass for her to take. She took it from his fingers, and he seemed to fall back to sleep. He'd not realized who she was, or even that she was there, and Siobhan realized that even if she spoke to him, he'd not remember.

Nonetheless, she had to try.

Wincing at the pain it caused, she lowered to the floor and touched his shoulder. "Miles. What's happening?"

He groaned, and barely opened his eyes. "You?" The word came out in a hoarse whisper. To her surprise, he immediately pulled her into a tight embrace, pushing his face into the crook of her neck. For a long moment, they remained like that, Miles with a desperate hold on her, moaning into her shoulder.

"Do you want to marry me?" Siobhan asked. "Are you this way because you are being forced to take me to wife?"

Miles' only response was a groan of pain. Then he slowly relaxed, drifting into what she thought was slumber; it was just as she'd fallen asleep after drinking her pain tincture. He would not be able to speak for a long while, and she realized it was best for her to return downstairs.

After placing a pillow under his head, Siobhan covered him with a blanket. Her heart broke for him, and rage surged that he was being left alone in this helpless, pained state. Still, there was little she could do or say without divulging that she had snuck into his room and seen him so exposed. She leaned forward and pressed a kiss to his parted lips.

"I will help you," she vowed softly. "I will return and help you."

Just as she arrived at the bottom floor, the same maid—who appeared to be waiting for her—motioned for her to turn away and to go out through a wide set of doors that led to the garden. Siobhan hurried out and settled gingerly onto the first bench she came to so she could rest after her exertions. As she sat, she was able to watch a nearby fountain. Usually, she'd find it quite relaxing, but her mind was full of worry for Miles. What had happened to him? Would he be all right? Maybe she could return to the house and ask the same maid who'd let her know where Miles would be.

She was still musing on this when her mother walked out and spotted her there. "There you are. Come back inside, Siobhan. We have a few last items to discuss that require your input."

"Yes, Mother," she answered. She'd have to find another way to determine what was wrong with Miles, and how she could help him.

CHAPTER TEN

S UNLIGHT ACROSS HIS face woke Miles and he slowly opened his eyes, scared it would trigger the pain again. To his relief the headache had gone as if it had never occurred.

He sat up, realizing he'd spent the night on the floor. He pushed away the blanket that had been placed over him. Probably by his mother, who now lay on his bed, still asleep.

She and his father took turns sleeping in the room whenever he had an episode. His heart warmed at knowing they refused to leave him alone even though the drops he took made him sleep deeply.

A vague memory of Siobhan being there came to him and he wondered if it had been a dream. There was no way she could have come there and been allowed to his bedchamber. Still, he could swear she'd been there. Perhaps it was a delusion brought on by the tincture, though that had never happened before.

His mother stirred, opening her eyes to meet his. "Thanks be to God," she stated in a groggy tone. "You are better."

"It seems so," he replied, stretching. "I am famished."

The duchess sat up, smiling at him. She reached for the cord that hung next to the bed. "Something can be brought at once."

When his valet entered, he ordered a bath. The man, Reynolds, gave him a warm look. "I am so glad to see you faring better, my lord. I will see that food is brought immediately."

"How many days have passed?" he asked.

"Surprisingly, only two," his mother replied. "Perhaps the

attacks will be shorter and soon disappear."

He didn't dare hope. However, on the rare occasions when the headaches lasted less than a sennight, he was glad for it.

The bathwater was a balm to his battered soul. Left alone with only his thoughts once again, Miles wondered at the vivid dream of Siobhan having visited him.

He could not fathom why the dream had been so real.

DESCENDING THE STAIRS, Miles went to find his father. They usually spent the mornings poring over ledgers to ensure every one of their many properties were accounted for. They owned lands in England and on the island in the West Indies from which his father hailed. Every one of their holdings was meticulously handled to ensure profits. Often, either he or his father would travel and visit their estates, something which Miles enjoyed.

With a look of relief, his father looked up from a ledger. "Ah, good to see you, son. Your mother told me you've gotten over the latest episode." He waved Miles into the room.

"I am still a bit disoriented," Miles said. "Each time, I feel as if I'm waking from a disturbing dream. My jaw aches from grinding my teeth."

He lowered himself into a chair opposite his father's large desk and looked to see which ledger he held. "I am eager to work and get back to the routine."

There was a flicker of something he didn't quite understand in his father's gaze and the duke looked away. "There is a matter we must discuss. We had company yesterday, midday."

By the crease between his father's brows, Miles knew it had to be something serious. "What happened?"

"It was the Blairs and their pretty daughter. Your mother has decided that you will marry her."

Miles started. Him? Marry? Siobhan? He opened his mouth to

protest, as he had many times before. But something stopped him, though he wasn't sure what it was.

His father continued without taking a breath. "What I mean to say is that your mother *and I* have decided. It is for the best. She is from a good family and seems of good temperament. I do believe to have heard you were acquainted with her before her unfortunate incident."

Miles could only stare silently at his father. Was he still delirious? Unable to speak, he inhaled sharply.

"Plans have commenced for an engagement gala, it seems." His father shook his head. "Both your mother and hers are a-tither with excitement."

Miles sat forward. "This was all decided yesterday?"

His father's wide shoulders lifted and lowered. "I do believe your mother had already decided it had to be. She got wind of the vicious rumors and decided an immediate stop would be put to them with an engagement. I am also sure she pounced on the state of affairs to ensure you get married." To Miles' surprise, his father began to laugh. "She's got you." The duke tried in vain not to continue laughing but failed. "I am sorry, son. Certainly you would not mind marriage to such a beauty."

"Father this is not comical. I should have a say in whom I marry." Miles found it strange that he did not feel as indignant as he sounded. "I barely know the woman. Besides, since when does Mother give credence to silly gossip?"

His father looked at the door and Miles turned to see his mother entering. Her face was bright as she looked at him. "I am so glad you are well, darling. We have much to do. As I'm sure your father has informed you, the Blairs came yesterday demanding you marry their daughter."

"And you had no choice but to agree," Miles stated dryly.

His mother gave a curt nod, her happy expression belying her words. "Indeed, your father and I had little choice. But you must admit that she is a delightful lass." Her Scots burr was accentuated by her excitement. "Oh Miles. She will be wearing lavender."

If not for the situation, Miles would have laughed. Lavender was his favorite color. Instead, he let out a long breath. "Have you considered that I do not wish to marry?" He'd told them this repeatedly. Of course, they were aware of his feelings. But apparently his desires about his own life were not enough to stop their desires that he should and must marry.

His mother turned away from him to appeal to his father. "Leon, explain to your son that an agreement has been forged. He *must* marry Siobhan Blair."

"I am sitting right here, Mother, *you* can explain it to me. How could I become engaged, when not present?" His tone was sharper than he'd intended, but he was becoming annoyed at the situation.

His father stood and gave him a pointed look. "Do not take that tone with your mother. An agreement has been made between our families. You will be getting married. Now, go to the tailor and have a suit made for the event."

"Ah yes." His mother was once again alight with joy. "The engagement gala will be next week."

HIS THREE FRIENDS were stunned into silence after Miles casually invited them to his engagement party. "A formal invitation will be coming, of course, but I wanted to ensure that as my closest friends you were aware before anyone else."

"This is rather sudden," Grant said, staring at him as if able to find something to hint as to what really happened. "I wasn't aware you were courting the lass."

"I wasn't," Miles said, not offering more of an explanation. In truth, he was quite enjoying the moment when his friends looked as blindsided as he'd felt earlier.

Evan narrowed his eyes and pursed his lips before stating, "You jest, to get a rise from us. Surely you, the ultimate confirmed bachelor, are not going to be marrying someone you've yet to court, much less bed."

"Did you bed her?" Henry asked, a look of disbelief on his handsome face. He turned to the others. "As to jesting, he called us here for an urgent meeting. If it is not about the ship, then I expect there is some truth to what he says."

Once again, they grew silent. "What happened?" Evan finally asked.

Miles informed them of the harrowing rescue, which they'd already heard about and then about her mother immediately starting the rumors in an effort to trap him into marriage. But he felt compelled to add, "Siobhan herself is adamant against being forced into marriage. She told me she'd never wish to marry someone against their will—at least, that's what she told me one of the last times we spoke."

He drank the last bit of his whiskey, and the glass was immediately refilled by Grant. "Continue."

"Then, our mothers got involved. Hers with the agenda of her daughter marrying well, of course, and mine glad to finally have the opportunity for grandchildren."

There was a clearing of throats as his friends fought not to laugh.

He shook his head and let his shoulders slump. "Go ahead and laugh. My own father seems to think the entire thing is humorous. Even though we're talking about marriage. It is the rest of my life. I honestly have a hard time finding it comical that I'm being pushed into a state of marriage without my permission or will."

Grant nodded. "Although I would never consider it as I am deeply in love with my wife, it is not uncommon for a man of your status to have a lover. So you *can* decide not to be confined to the marriage bed only."

Miles frowned. "I would not cheat on my wife. Why would you think I would? Do *you* think I would?" Did his friends have such a low opinion of his integrity? Did *he*? He was growing confused and considered that perhaps he should return to his townhouse and spend time alone in thought.

"I do not think you would if you were happily married." Henry motioned around the room. "No one here even considers it. But we all married for love, not because we were forced into an arrangement."

The words sprang to his lips before he had time to even consider them. "What if I love Siobhan? What say you then?"

His friends stared at him with varying expressions of surprise. Miles himself was stunned by his declaration. "I mean…I *could* fall in love," he finished in a less than convincing tone.

The idea surprised him, and he thought of little else as he finished his drink and started for home.

WHEN HE ARRIVED at his townhouse, Jones greeted him. "Sir, I am glad to see you are faring better. We were informed you've been unwell."

"Thank you, Jones," he stated. "Is there anything pressing I must see to?"

"Not at the moment," Jones replied. "Should I send for your valet?"

Miles considered that there was to be planning at his family home and wondered whether he should be there or not. "Let me think about it. I am not sure whether I will remain here or at the family estate."

He'd just removed his overcoat and was just in shirt and pants when Jones appeared at his bedchamber doorway. "My lord, you have a visitor."

"Who?" He was not in the mood for company. The last thing he needed at the moment was to have some sort of social conversation. "Never mind. Tell whoever it is that I am indisposed."

"Very good, my lord. I will inform Miss Blair—."

He held up his hand. "Siobhan Blair?"

"Yes, my lord." Although his butler kept his expressionless and impartial mask in place, Miles sensed that like everyone else, Jones found humor in the situation. The thought annoyed him and yet—he could see the humor in the situation, he supposed.

If he chose, that is. "I will see her." Not wanting to hear anything else, he rounded the butler and went to the front room.

Siobhan stood next to the window, a picture of serenity as she peered out. It was surprising to see her standing. Wearing a morning gown in the shade of sunset orange, gloves, and with a small hat perched on her head, she looked every bit a lady. Which she was, of course.

"You came alone?" He asked, looking around the room.

She whirled around, taking him in head to foot. "I didn't believe it when my friend Henriette told me she saw you riding past earlier this morning. You are well?"

"What do you mean?" He walked closer. "Why would I not be?"

Her gaze slid sideways as she seemed to consider what to say next. "Your mother said you had left for England."

"I arrived late last night." He looked around the room. "After all that has occurred, I am surprised you'd dare to come here alone."

Siobhan motioned to the window. "My maid and Henriette are outside. I only wished to stop for a moment to speak to you. Are you aware our mothers—well, our parents—have decided we are to marry?"

Her vivid clear blue eyes met his and Miles took her in. She was indeed the most beautiful woman he'd ever met. Every time he saw her, it took his breath away and he noticed something new to admire in her. Today it was petal pink lips that were currently slightly parted and enticing as she waited for his response.

"I am aware. Father told me early this morning. It seems all agreements have been made. Were you there?" He wondered if perhaps his dream had occurred while she was there at his home. Of course, he had no concept of time.

"I was." She tapped his forearm. "Miles, I want you to know that I would never wish to force you into marriage. Perhaps if you speak to your mother, there can be a way to disentangle all of this."

For a moment, he was stunned into silence. Siobhan didn't wish to marry him. Although he'd spoken against it, he'd not expected that she would try to find a way to break the engagement.

"I do not believe we can change the course of things." He looked away, afraid she'd see the disappointment in his eyes and surprised that the feeling had permeated his heart.

"I am truly sorry," Siobhan said, taking a step, then two, closer. "Are you cross with me?"

He met her gaze. "Of course not. I suppose this is my doing for bringing you here and putting you in this predicament."

A look of confusion crossed her features. "Then will you be there?"

"At the engagement gala, yes." He paused to take in her beauty. "I have been instructed to visit the tailor for a suit to match your lavender dress."

Her cheeks turned pink, and he could not stop himself from reaching for her. He put his arms around her. "If there was a way to stop all of this, I would," he finally said. "I do not wish to cause you a life of regret."

She looked into his eyes, searchingly. "Will I cause you a life of regret?"

"I think not."

Unable to keep from it, he kissed her, doing his best to convey his newly-discovered feelings for her and praying that one day, she would feel the same for him. Never in his life had he been in love and more surprisingly, he hadn't expected to be. He'd always been able to easily disengage his emotions from any physical attraction, but for some reason it was all but impossible now.

Just holding her against him, time spun faster, and his head and heart were lighter.

He deepened the kiss, and she grasped his shirt, making him envision that soon she would be able to touch his bare skin.

When Siobhan moaned, lifting her right-hand and combing her fingers through his hair, he wanted to shout for joy. Even if she didn't love him, she was definitely not immune to his touch.

"If you do not go now, I will be unable to stop kissing you," Miles murmured against her lips. "I will call on you tomorrow. We should be seen out in public as the invitations arrive at households."

He pressed one last lingering kiss to her lips, and straightened, noting the darkening of her eyes. "Very well. Until tomorrow." Her response was breathless.

"Siobhan," Miles said, stopping her as she went to pass him. "Just so you know. I am not sorry to be marrying you."

Her lips curved into a smile, just a bit. "Neither am I."

If not for Jones appearing and standing by the door, he would have wrapped her in his arms and whirled her in a circle. "Until tomorrow then."

For a long moment, she stared into his eyes. It was as if she wished to say something, but could not. Finally, she nodded and walked out.

He stood at the window watching the coachman assist her into an open-air carriage. There two women waited for her, one he recognized as her French friend who had accompanied her to the slum on Saturday mornings. He hoped her incident had impressed upon her the danger that going there alone exposed her to; as her husband, it would be up to him to keep her safe from now on. He was up to the task.

SIOBHAN FOUND IT impossible to sit still. The entire morning, she'd tried to distract herself, but nothing worked. Even when Charles came to call on Amelia, the short distraction barely helped. With a flushed face and bright expression, Amelia had appeared, wearing a soft yellow morning gown that suited her fair complexion. It made Siobhan happy to see her sister finally finding a suitor about whom she was excited. As they'd left for a carriage ride with their shared personal maid, Siobhan stood watch until the carriage disappeared.

Mind awhirl, she'd turned to face the room, wondering what she and Miles would do when he came to call. He'd said that afternoon and confirmed it by sending a calling card which was delivered that morning. Such formality. She'd not ever thought about what life would be like for someone of his class. She'd never had a reason to.

Her mother, of course, could barely contain her enthusiasm. Already, she'd sent out invitations for tea, so that she could brag of Siobhan's engagement to the honorable Lord Miles. Not just that, but to emphasize that her daughter would be a duchess one day.

As for Siobhan, she would prefer if Miles were not titled. Even if he were the son of a simple lord would have been better for her, she supposed. The prospect of becoming a duchess was a daunting one and honestly, she had decided she would begin praying for his parents to live long lives, well into their hundreds, so she'd not have to worry about carrying such an exalted title.

A carriage pulled up, the Johnstone seal prominent on the door, and her heart began thundering against her breastbone. It was an open-air carriage, which she knew was because they had to be seen.

"Mother," Siobhan called out. "Who will chaperone me?"

Her mother rushed into the room and to the window. "Oh dear. I assumed he would come later, and Amelia would be back."

"Instead of a carriage ride, we can picnic in the garden," Siobhan suggested, glad not to have to be out in public. "I actually prefer it."

"That will not do. You must be seen." Her mother went to the doorway just as the butler appeared.

"Lord Miles," he announced as Miles walked up behind the man.

He greeted her mother, who acted as if King George himself visited. "My lord, please come in and make yourself comfortable." Her mother motioned to a maid, who'd been instructed to present herself swiftly upon Miles' appearance. "Lucille, see about refreshments for his lordship."

"There is no need," Miles said, sliding a look to Siobhan, who'd not had the opportunity to do more than nod in greeting. "I prefer to leave now and make the most of the pretty day."

"I do not have a chaperone," Siobhan said. "We may have to…" Penelope waved from the carriage.

Miles stated. "She insisted on coming."

Siobhan returned to the window and indeed, the pretty sprite and another young woman were in the carriage. Her lips curved. It was the twosome who'd gotten themselves in trouble at the ball. "Good. I am happy to see them."

Her mother looked disappointed. "Perhaps you can partake in refreshments upon your return."

Once in the carriage, Siobhan was grateful for the young women, whose presence would keep any awkwardness at bay.

"I hope you do not mind that Corrine and I wished to join you. We were bored senseless," Penelope said by way of greeting.

"I think Lord Miles is cross at us for coming," Corrine accused. "But her grace insisted he bring us."

Siobhan could not help but giggle, noticing Miles gave his sister and friend a droll look. "I normally would not mind. However, this is our first outing, and I'd hoped for more privacy."

He covered Siobhan's hand with his, sending shivers up her arm. Both girl's eyes widened, and they exchanged looks.

"Pretend we are not here," Penelope instructed, her eyes

pinned to their hands.

Miles shook his head and chuckled.

As expected, they drew much attention, with people greeting them and then whispering to companions as soon as they passed. Siobhan, Penelope, and Corrine spent the time counting how many people began to chatter about them. Instead of feeling awkward and uncomfortable at the public scrutiny, the girls made it fun. When people greeted them, they heard the girls' giggles after they'd passed, which in turn caused more curious looks.

At returning to her home, Miles walked her to the door, his gaze lingering on hers overly long. Siobhan herself found it hard to tear her eyes from him. There was a playful quiver on his lips.

"We will have time alone soon enough," he stated, bringing heat to her cheeks. "All the time we wish."

"I still cannot believe we are to marry. Are you sure not to be troubled?" Siobhan searched his face, hoping to read if he was truthful in his reply.

He let out a breath. "I had not planned to marry yet. In truth, if left to my own devices, I wouldn't marry until old and gray. That being said, rest assured, I am pleased to marry you, Siobhan."

Unsure if his reply made her feel better, all she managed in answer was to nod and smile. "I will see you at the engagement gala then?"

His brows drew together. "Yes." He leaned forward and placed a soft kiss to her lips. It was quite forward to do it in plain view of anyone passing. The street was deserted, the only witnesses, two giggling girls staring at them in wide-eyed fascination.

CHAPTER ELEVEN

Two Months later…

"YOU LOOK BEAUTIFUL," Amelia stated walking in a circle around Siobhan. "I am truly happy for you."

The wedding gown was not as elaborate as most brides' since Siobhan preferred simpler designs. But in her opinion, it was perfect. The bodice was snug, with a square neckline that flattered her full chest. From the waist, the skirts flowed to the floor in waves of white satin and lace. Her ebony tresses were pulled up and away from her face, into a simple but beautiful upsweep that allowed for her curls to cascade down past Siobhan's shoulders.

In truth, she found it hard to recognize the woman in the mirror. Her sky-blue eyes shone with excitement and nerves, and her cheeks were naturally pinkened by all the activities of preparation.

She turned from side to side, loving the way the skirts swung. "I feel beautiful."

There was a discreet knock on the door and a maid peered in. "It is time."

Both Amelia and her mother rushed to Siobhan, reaching out as if to tug her, but then drawing back unsure how to usher her forward.

"I will not escape," Siobhan assured them. "Do not fret."

Her mother gave her a suspicious look. "I will ensure you will not by not leaving your side until you are standing beside Lord

Miles at the front of the church."

THE CHURCH WASN'T far. They'd decided to marry at her family's church instead of the chapel on the Johnstone estate. The celebration after their service would be at the estate, however.

As if she were in a dream, Siobhan could barely feel her feet touch the ground as she walked through the front entrance of the large, ornate church. Her father approached and presented his arm to her. Immediately her eyes stung with happy tears and Siobhan pressed her lips together in an effort to keep from crying.

"Now, do not cry, we will look foolish sobbing through our walk." Her father's eyes were bright with emotion. "Let us give you away, dear lass."

Somehow she managed to make the long trek to the front of the church without falling apart. The entire time, she kept her eyes on Miles. Dressed in cream and white, he was—as always—perfection, a beautiful man. With each step closer to him, Siobhan became more certain that he was the only man for her. He was the beginning and end of everything she'd ever desired.

Although he seemed relaxed by outward appearances, upon nearing, she noticed how he swallowed visibly every so often. She smiled at him, hoping to convey with her eyes that all would be well. That she would strive to make him happy and that he'd never regret having to marry her.

The vicar's words flowed over her like a warm breeze, every syllable filling her heart as they repeated the vows.

It seemed but a minute before they were walking out of the church greeted with cheers and showers of flower petals. Many from the area had gathered outside the church to catch a glimpse of the woman who'd managed to ensnare the most eligible bachelor in Glasgow. Prying curious eyes boring into Siobhan dissecting everything about her.

Finally, they were settled in the carriage, which she was grateful was an enclosed one and rode off toward the Johnstone estate.

"Finally alone," Miles said, taking her hands and kissing her knuckles. "How do you feel?"

"Breathless," Siobhan replied searching his face. "You?"

Instead of a reply, he wrapped his arms around her shoulders and hugged her. "I am not sure."

The reply was honest, and she should have been grateful that he did not lie. However, her chest tightened because he'd not said something more positive.

Unfortunately, it was the first of more disappointments to come that evening.

"Congratulations," a couple she didn't recognize said, seeming to be sincere in their well wishes. Siobhan was exhausted by all the fake congratulatory greetings that night. People had wished them many years of happiness while scrutinizing Siobhan as if she were an insect they'd never seen before. Down their noses, more times than she could count, women had informed her how fortunate she was.

The unasked question swirled in the air around her like a thick fog. "Why you?"

She hurried to a balcony for fresh air and hoping that from there she could catch a glimpse of Miles. Sometime earlier, they'd been pulled in opposite directions by guests, and she'd not spoken to him in at least an hour.

"How are you faring?" It was Miles' mother, the duchess, who'd walked out to speak to her. "I can understand these things can be overwhelming."

Siobhan nodded. "I want to remember my wedding day as a time of happy moments, surrounded by family and close friends. This is so much more." She left the sentence at that, not wishing to offend Miles' mother. "I appreciate all you've done to make this… day such a success."

The duchess' lips curved. "You are definitely a good match for my son. He is perturbed that there are so many people here. I explained to him just as I am informing you—with our status in society, we must keep a tight rein. My husband and son are of another race than most of society and we must behave and keep a strict life that is above reproach. Although I do not consider our hold on things to be tenuous, I do think it is imperative we do things to appease others, despite our own inner desires."

What the woman said made sense. Still, Siobhan did not find it fair. As it was obvious her new mother-in-law lived by the just-spoken rules, Siobhan wasn't sure she would ever aspire to keep to such a strict way of life. Whether one lived perfectly or not, if the fickle people of society wished it so, all could be dashed in but a moment.

They re-entered the room and she scanned it from one side to the other. As they walked to be greeted by yet another group of strangers, Siobhan could still not find Miles. Finally, she was able to tear herself away and she walked to where her mother and father were.

"They make a stunning couple, do not you think?" Her mother asked, watching Amelia and Charles dance. "Do you not agree, dear?"

She followed her mother's line of sight to a flushed Amelia smiling brightly at her partner as they whirled in circles around the dance floor. "Yes, they are lovely. But, Mother, I cannot seem to find Miles. Where is my husband?"

⟫⟫⟫⟪⟪⟪

IN THE LIBRARY, Miles had finally found a bit of privacy. A light throb behind his eyes warned of things to come. "Not tonight," he murmured, pressing two fingers on each side of his head. He'd managed to make it through social events before while suffering from his headaches. Usually he'd been able to make excuses for an early departure before rushing to his bedchamber where he'd lock himself in for days.

Things were different now. He was married and his wife expected a wedding night. As much as he imagined being with her and making the beauty his, it was hard to fathom making love while suffering the blinding pain.

"There he is." Evan, followed by Grant and Henry walked in. "The groom."

Miles' lips curved at their expressions of disbelief. "Surely, you believe me now." He motioned to chairs. "Please sit, I will pour."

Welcoming the distraction, he poured his friends brandy recently imported from one of his family's properties, not taking any for himself as he'd found it sometimes exacerbated the ill-effects of his affliction.

His friends were aware he suffered from the horrible head-aches as they'd spent time together in boarding school and later often spent summers together at the Johnstone country house.

Evan studied him. "You do not feel well?"

There was no use in denying it. "I do not. I have no idea how I will make it through the night. I am afraid my bride may be disappointed in there not being a wedding night on the actual wedding night." Miles gave up all pretense and sunk into a chair. Closing his eyes gave some respite and he massaged his temples.

"You should tell her," Henry said. "It is best she know."

Without opening his eyes, he leaned back into the chair. "That she's married a sick man? I prefer to wait. But if she asks, I will use the excuse of drinking too much."

This time Grant spoke. "If it only lasts a day, you can use that excuse. However, the headaches usually last longer. I am sure the excitement and stress of the wedding brought it on."

Miles nodded. "Second time in a couple of months. It has never happened so close together before."

Someone squeezed his shoulder; the act made him feel worse. That he was pitied for an ailment that he could not control was one thing, but that he could not perform husbandly duties on his wedding night was not something he would ever forgive himself for. "I will get through it. I refuse to allow this to control me." He bit out the words and took a breath. "Let us rejoin our wives."

The three sets of eyes met his, each filled with warmth that came from years of true friendship.

"Whatever we can do to help, we will," Henry said.

When they walked into the ballroom, he went directly to Siobhan, who smiled at him brightly. She studied him for a moment before she spoke. "Your mother is so kind. She's explained to me already things I must know about life with your family without making me feel inadequate."

"She is a good woman. I believe you will become good friends," Miles replied.

"I believe so as well," Siobhan replied. "And, I believe we should dance again."

He led her to the dance floor, everyone watching as they waltzed around the room. Soon other couples joined them as the fast melody filled the room, flowing through the air. Siobhan was a good partner, light on her feet and seeming to enjoy the music. He was glad that although neither of them cared for large gatherings, she could perform the duties required without fault. There was a pleased smile on her face as they walked from the dance floor and were greeted by an older couple who were more interested in finding out about the possible impropriety of their relationship than to congratulate them.

"This was certainly a whirlwind romance," the woman said, her gaze sweeping from him to Siobhan.

"It was," Siobhan replied breathlessly. "I am so glad we didn't have a long courtship."

Miles pressed a kiss to his wife's temple. "I could not fathom being apart from this beauty, and using the rumors as an excuse convinced her and her family that we should marry quickly. I must find out who started the false accusations and thank them."

The couple's brows shot up, the woman recovering first.

"You have such a fresh perspective of how things should be done. Bravo."

There was a clinking of glasses, and everyone turned to find Evan, Grant, and Henry, along with their wives, standing on the stairwell. Seeing them together made his heart squeeze. They held up glasses, as champagne flutes were pushed into his and Siobhan's hands.

Henry cleared his throat as the crowd quieted. "I speak on behalf of Grant and Wren Murray, Evan and Felicity McLeod, as well as Hannah and myself, to wish our dearest childhood friend Miles and his beautiful bride, Siobhan, a heartfelt congratulations. We wish you the best life has to offer."

With a hearty chuckle, Grant elbowed Henry aside. "The four of us, once rogues, have been tamed by women who not only changed our way but stole our hearts. Siobhan, welcome to our family."

Evan stepped in front of Grant. "Since they said something, I must add this for Miles. Through everything, you have always been the steadfast one, the cornerstone of our group. Because of that, I want to tell everyone present. Miles Johnstone is a man of honor and the best ally any man, or woman, could ever ask for."

Miles had to blink the moisture away from his eyes; he took a breath and lifted his glass in response.

Henry held up a hand. "Now I believe we should excuse the bride and groom from the festivities so they can start their happily ever after."

There were gasps of shock from the women and chuckles from the men.

Miles needed no other encouragement. The headache was inevitable, but it wasn't as bad yet as he knew it would become. He lifted Siobhan into his arms and headed to the stairwell as applause and cheers erupted.

CHAPTER TWELVE

"IN A FANTASY, I would throw you upon the bed and ravage you," Miles said when he carried her into his room and plopped her down on her feet. "However, it would be impossible to remove so much." He motioned to her attire.

Siobhan eyed him, taking in how handsome he was, unsure how to proceed as she had no ideas of what she was supposed to do on the wedding night.

She and Henriette had pored through books and interrogated married maids to know how exactly men and women made love.

Blushing furiously, one maid had told them all about the male appendage and how it became hard when the man became aroused. When their mouths fell open at her describing that the man entered the woman, she'd insisted it was enjoyable. Siobhan had her doubts.

Both she and Henriette had had nightmares that night and had vowed to stay away from men. However, their curiosity got the best of them and soon they'd corralled Susan's neighbor, who helped the sick woman. The woman had entered the apartment sharing about a wonderful night with her husband one morning while Susan and the children were napping.

The woman described the same thing as the maid, yet with much more detail. By the time she was done, all three of them were breathless.

The thought of joining with Miles drove her between excitement and fear. What if the women had lied and it was not going to be enjoyable?

"I need help removing all of this," Siobhan said when he carried her into the room and plopped her down on her feet.

"Come closer." Miles's eyes darkened, and her breath caught. Was he aroused? As curious as she was, Siobhan didn't dare look down at the front of his breeches.

Instead of beginning the task of undressing her, Miles let his mouth cover hers. The kiss was soft and still, it rendered her thoughtless. While he kissed her and murmured words she'd be hard-pressed to remember, his fingers glided over the buttons on the back of the dress. Lips dancing across hers, she lost track of time and was surprised when her dress slipped from her shoulders, and past her waist to puddle at her feet.

It was a matter of minutes before he helped her remove all the bothersome underclothing. When left only in a light chemise, she stilled his hands with hers.

"What about you?" Her voice was breathless, her chest lifting and lowering keeping up with her racing pulse.

Miles took a step backward and without taking his eyes from her, he removed first his waistcoat, then his cravat. She'd seen him in this state of undress at his townhouse, and yet, at the moment it seemed so much more intimate.

When he sat to remove his shoes, it occurred to her she still wore her slippers, so together they removed their footwear. He straightened, removed his shirt, and slid the breeches from his narrow hips.

Unlike her dress on the floor, he lay his clothes on a chair, then—naked as the day he was born—he picked up her dress and placed it over the other clothing.

Siobhan could not tear her regard away from his body. He was sleek and muscular at the same time. Unlike her blossomed chest, his was broad, but flat, and his stomach was as well. Unable to keep from it, she finally studied his maleness, and her eyes widened.

It was just as the women had described. It lifted under her

scrutiny, seeming to come to life. Hardening and thickening, the staff jutted from his body.

"Let us do away with the last of your clothing. I want to see all of you," Miles murmured, moving closer. He reached for the hem of the featherlight item and pulled it up and over her head.

At this point, she could not formulate words. Unsure whether it was panic or just nerves, her hands trembled when she reached up to remove her hair adornment.

"Relax," Miles said, bringing her against him, the touch of his skin a warm balm, his lips trailing across her shoulder and weakening her knees.

"Oh." The word escaped her when his hands cupped her bottom, bringing her against the hardness of his shaft. It was wonderful, the way their bodies melded. His touches were enjoyable and every single one of her senses seemed sharper all of a sudden.

Miles lifted her and carried her to the bed. Just as he leaned to place her upon it, Siobhan noticed a slight grimace on his face, but it was quickly gone.

Without hesitation, he joined her, coming over her and pushing her legs apart with his knee. "This first time will be a bit uncomfortable," he informed her in a tone that was without inflection. "I promise to make every instance after this enjoyable."

Siobhan gulped in a breath as he fell upon her, his mouth on hers and hand trailing past her stomach, to her thigh, and finally, between her legs.

She tensed when his fingers slid between her sex, only to start when he touched a spot that sent jolts of sensations from her head to her toes. The more the caresses continued, the harder it became to focus until she was writhing under Miles. Suddenly it was as if she fell into a warm pool of water. In a strange, but beautiful way, her senses overcome, every inch of Siobhan's body coming to life.

Miles drove into her, his manhood seeming too wide for her entrance, the realization of what had occurred bringing her slowly back to reality just as a piercing pain struck her inside.

"Ouch!" Siobhan screamed, pushing at his hips in an effort to dislodge him. "It hurts."

"Shh." Miles pressed his lips near her ear. "It will pass."

The awareness of being joined as husband and wife sunk in and tears sprang to her eyes. The pain ebbed, gradually being replaced by a sense of wonder. "We did it," she whispered. "We are one at this moment." There was awe in her voice. "I wondered what it would feel like, and now I know."

He chuckled, kissing her lips. "Yes, my beautiful wife. Indeed we are. Are you still in pain?"

Despite herself, she felt her face burn. "No. Not anymore."

Moving slowly, he drew out and then back in, each movement seeming measured as he continued to drive in and out of her.

It was interesting, what he did. Siobhan studied him, not sure what her role was, but liking that he seemed intent on continuing. Moments later, a sliver of pleasing sensations filled her, and she warmed to the notion that during these times, there was no one else but them.

Miles became breathless his movements more frantic, and Siobhan ran her hands down his back which was slick with perspiration.

He tensed, and let out a sensual groan. When he collapsed over her, Miles was breathless. Still joined, he lifted his head and kissed her.

After a few moments, he rolled to lay beside her, and Siobhan studied his profile. "You are so very handsome."

His bark of laughter made her smile. Miles turned to face her. "If you stopped thinking so much, it would have been more enjoyable for you."

"I was waiting for it to hurt again," Siobhan replied. "Try enjoying yourself while waiting for another stab of pain."

His lips pressed to the tip of her nose. "I should have told you. It only hurts once."

Screwing up her face, she huffed. "Yes, you should have. Nonetheless, it was very nice."

"If not for you being so adorable, my ego would be bruised," Miles informed her.

She snuggled against him, his arms around her. In his arms, as his wife, Siobhan knew she'd been gifted something special. A wonderful ever-after.

The day's activities claimed her, and she fell into a deep slumber.

⟫⟫⟩✦⟨⟪⟪

IN THE MORNING, Siobhan woke to maids bringing in a tub and water. She sat up in the bed and looked at the opposite—empty— side of the bed.

Hot and cool water were poured into the tub and then instructed by the head maid, perfumed oils were added. The woman gave her a wide smile. "I am Leena and will be at your disposal from now on. I will have tea and toast brought in. Is there anything else you require?"

The woman looked to be in her thirties, with a pleasant face and light brown hair that was pulled up under a cap.

"Where is Lord Miles?"

Leena slid a look to the doorway. "In his bedchamber, my lady."

It was then she looked around the room. It was devoid of any personal belongings and not the room she'd seen Miles in the night she'd snuck upstairs. When had he left?

"I see. Thank you."

Feeling a bit unsettled, she allowed Leena to help her into the bath. While she bathed, the woman laid out her clothes. "I will see about your tea and return to help you dress and to fix your hair, my lady."

She'd have to get used to being addressed with a title. But it was the least of her concerns. What she really wanted to know was—where was her husband?

WHEN SHE JOINED the duke, duchess and Penelope for breakfast, Miles was noticeably absent. Siobhan sat across from Penelope after greeting Miles' parents.

"If you wish to eat anything different, just inform the cook," Arabella, Miles' mother, said.

"Everything is perfect," Siobhan replied, sliding a look to the doorway. "Will Miles be joining us?"

Penelope frowned. "He is…"

"He will not," Arabella interrupted. "Miles prefers his own company some days. We are used to it, I am sure you will be as well, in time."

Siobhan nodded, saying nothing but looking at Penelope who seemed to find her plate of food most interesting. She'd find out the truth from the lass, Siobhan had no doubt, since she was young and open.

Finally by the afternoon and with Miles nowhere to be seen, she was becoming annoyed. It was understandable that someone would wish for private time, however, he'd left her without telling her anything. Would they live there at the estate, or his townhouse? What did he expect her to do day-to-day?

There was the matter of her excursions to help the shelter and Susan. She'd planned to talk to him about continuing it. Despite the attack and the fact that no one had located the scoundrel, they'd insist Jean-Paul remain with them the entire time.

The work was much too precious to her to simply give it up.

"This is nice," Penelope said with a smile as they walked through the garden. Siobhan used the excuse of cutting flowers to get time alone with the lass.

"Yes it is." Siobhan looked at the house. "Is your brother still in his bedchamber?"

"Or in the study," Penelope said. "He is so boring."

Siobhan could not help but smile. "I do not think to have ever considered him to be a bore. Miles seems vibrant and always in motion."

"I mean he always wants to work. He and Papa pore over those ledgers of theirs, day after day. They scribble items into them, then talk about what they wrote. When visitors come, they go to the study and also seem interested in the ledgers. It is such a tedious thing, do not you think?"

"Agreed. However, I am told your family's holdings are vast and require much oversight. My father informed me that your father and Miles are responsible for entire villages and many people's livelihoods."

"I suppose," Penelope replied, seeming not interested. "I am glad you married my brother. Perhaps it will help him."

The statement made Siobhan stop. "Help him?"

Penelope's face brightened. "Corrine is here!" She turned toward the house.

"Help him with what?" Siobhan insisted.

The young lass pressed her lips together as she considered her reply. "To not be so boring." With that, she shoved the basket into Siobhan's hands and hurried away.

AT SUPPERTIME, AGAIN Miles was absent. Siobhan refrained from asking about him this time as she expected to receive the same reply. Hopefully he would come to see her in her bedchamber. She had so many questions.

"Dear?" Her mother-in-law brought her out of her musings. "Is something wrong with the food?"

Siobhan realized she held her morsel in the air away from the plate and not quite to her mouth.

"No, not at all. I was deep in thought. I'm just wondering what my role will be, here. And, if we are to remain here."

The duke and duchess exchanged looks. The duke spoke, his West Indies accent as rich as his deep voice. "It will be up to you and my son as to where you decide to live."

The duchess added, "I believe the townhouse to be a good place for a bachelor. Without a large garden and such, you would be kept indoors most of the day. Here, there are plenty of rooms, gardens, and a forest to ride in and explore. There is also a pond not too far, a perfect place for picnics."

Siobhan took what they said into consideration. "It *is* beautiful here."

Evening came and Leena left the bedchamber after wishing her a good night. Siobhan paced the floor, anxious to see Miles. When after a long while he didn't appear, she decided to seek him out. Preferring his own company was one thing, but leaving her alone for an entire day right after their wedding seemed ridiculous.

Opening the door slowly, she felt like a thief when peering out into the silent house. She tip-toed to the same room she'd gone to before and didn't bother knocking. Thankfully, the door didn't creak when she pushed it open just enough to slip in.

Miles stood leaning against the window looking down into the dark garden. One hand up to his forehead, the other on the window's frame.

"Miles," Siobhan said in a soft but firm tone. "Why have you stayed away all day?" She walked closer. There wasn't even a candle to light the room; the only soft brightness came from moonlight.

"No." He whirled to face her, his face shadowed. "Leave at once." His menacing tone made her angrier.

"I will not until you talk to me." Siobhan straightened her spine. "Answer me."

Miles moved so fast that before she knew it, he'd grasped her arm and walked her back to the door. "Do not ever come here until invited. *Never.*"

In vain, she tried to see his face. "Why are you acting this way?"

He inhaled deeply, and she waited for a reply. Instead, he opened the door and shoved her out. The clicking of the latch seemed to echo in the silence as she stood there in shock.

Who had she married?

CHAPTER THIRTEEN

"WHAT DAY IS it?" Miles asked his valet. Finally the pain had receded after what he thought was a day or two.

"Saturday, my lord," Reynold replied. "You have been cloistered since your wedding."

An entire week.

His breath caught. "And Siobhan? Has she been well?"

"Yes, my lord. The lady has gone for a ride with your mother and sister, she's been to visit her family, and has spent many an hour in the garden."

He met the man's gaze in the mirror. "I should have known the short one was only a prelude of what was to come. I've left my bride on her own since our wedding. I am sure she is not impressed with the husband she's been allotted."

The valet remained silent, brushing the shoulders and back of his surcoat. Finally the man spoke. "If I may suggest my lord, perhaps time alone with your wife may be in order."

Reynolds was happily married to Leena, Siobhan's new personal maid. Their wedding had been a simple, yet enjoyable affair which Miles had gladly attended. Now a year later, they remained quite content.

When he entered the dining room, only his father was about, his eyes brightening at seeing him. "I am glad to see you faring better. There is much to discuss. A shipment from the London property has been lost."

While Miles ate, they discussed business, but the entire time, he kept an eye on the door. Finally, he asked, "Where are the women?"

"They went to some sort of breakfast at the church. I do believe it has something to do with planning a celebration."

He was glad to hear that his mother had kept Siobhan entertained, while at the same time he'd hoped to see her. There was much to discuss, and he had to make his absence up to her.

"You have not told her?" his father asked. "You should."

Miles nodded. "I know. I'd hoped to spare her the knowledge of my shortcomings until after a few months together."

"Your headaches have been farther apart. But I agree the timing of this one was inopportune. Still, she should have been informed. The lass seems saddened by your absence."

As if he wasn't feeling enough guilt, the words were heavy on his shoulders. "I will speak with her upon her return."

❯❯❯❯❮❮❮❮

"GOOD MORNING, YOUR Lordship," Leena greeted him as he went to the French doors in search of much needed fresh air.

"Leena," he replied. "A word."

The woman smiled politely, waiting for what he'd say.

"How was my wife this morning?"

"She was quite excited, my lord. And she informed me that her works for the poor have always been satisfying and fulfilling."

He frowned. "I hope she is not disappointed. I do not think the celebration planned at the church that Mother took her to will be for the poor."

It was Leena's turn to frown. "Church, my lord?"

"My wife, she went with mother and my sister to the church this morning."

Leena relaxed. "No. She left just after then. A carriage came to get her. I believe the crest was a Perot."

His blood ran cold. "Who came for her?"

"A young lady and gentleman, my lord."

Glad to be already wearing his riding boots, he raced out and down the steps. When he neared the stables, one of the stable hands came out into the yard. "My lord?"

"Prepare my horse, Vance, at once."

Soon after, he raced from the estate, urging his horse to a gallop until reaching the city streets where he was forced to pull the beast to a trot.

Finally, he arrived at the market; he looked for her, but she was not there. So he dismounted and hurried to the shelter. A harried woman met him at the doorway, her tired expression softening at seeing him. "My lord. We here are so grateful for your presence and the saving of the young miss."

He attempted to keep his temper in check. "I am grateful as well. Have you seen her this morning?"

"Oh, aye. She was here much earlier. I presume she and Miss Henriette are over at the apartments to see about a sick woman named Susan and her bairns." She gave him an exhausted smile. "Saintly work, my lord."

He pulled out his purse and poured the contents into the shocked woman's hands. "For whatever is needed here at the shelter. And ensure to purchase something for yourself as well," he told her.

"Th-thank you... my lord." Her eyes shone with tears. "May you be blessed."

Although the anger dimmed, worry still filled Miles as he made his way to the apartments. Just as he neared, Siobhan, Henriette and her brother emerged. The women talked to each other while the man glanced around, his hands loose at his sides. It was apparent he was on guard for any possible approaches— today, anyway. As soon as they exited the building, the coachman appeared behind.

It was obvious they'd taken precautions; however, it didn't bode well that she'd returned to the place where she'd been attacked without informing his family. Or him, for that matter.

"Siobhan." His voice seemed to echo around them. "Come with me at once."

She swung toward him, wide-eyed and with her lips opened in surprise. A moment later, she scowled. "I will not."

As she hurried toward the waiting carriage and stepped up onto the box to climb in, Miles caught up with her. He pulled her down from the box, and threw her over his shoulder.

Siobhan let out a surprised squeal, while her companions and the coachman looked on with astonished looks.

"Do not interfere," Miles tore out when Henriette took a step toward them. "I will take my wife home."

It was a struggle as Siobhan did not help, but he managed to get her on the horse. They rode in silence for a few moments, then he could no longer keep silent.

"Why would you return there? The man has not been found as yet and could still yet be on the prowl for your return."

His stubborn wife sat upright between his legs, arms crossed and leaning away from him. If not for his arms around her to hold the horse's reins, she would topple off.

"Do you wish to fall off a horse again?" Miles snapped. "Lean back."

She did as told but her mouth was not quiet and did not comply. "I am not a prisoner. It is inappropriate for me to be seen astride a horse!"

"You are free to go as you please, to visit your friends and family. However, I will not allow you to return to that place."

The less than ladylike huff was her only reply. They rode past a group of women who stopped talking to stare at them. Siobhan glared at them. If not for being annoyed at her, he would have laughed at the women, who exchanged confused looks.

Upon their arrival at his parents' estate, he pulled the horse to a stop in front of the house and dismounted. He held up his arms to his reluctant bride, and she finally acquiesced to allow his assistance. The feel of her body against his palms brought him an immediate picture of her beneath him on their wedding night.

The woman was as beautiful without a stitch of clothing as she was at this very moment, fully dressed and spitting mad.

If he could ignite in flames from the looks she directed toward him, Miles was sure he would be totally consumed. "We should talk..." he began. Before he could finish the sentence, Siobhan whirled, lifted her skirts, and raced into the house.

He followed behind. Siobhan hurried past his father who'd come out of his study to see what occurred.

"She's a bit cross," Miles explained, heading up the stairs to see where Siobhan headed. If she reached the bedchamber before him and locked the door, any possibility of talking to her would be dashed, so he ran.

Just as she slipped into the room, he stopped her from slamming the door with his booted foot. Siobhan's expression turned to rage.

"Go away." She turned away from him.

"I must speak with you, and you will listen."

Her hands curled into fists. "Do not talk to me as if I am your child. Ordering me about. Ignoring me! I will not have it." To emphasize her point, she made a slashing motion across the air. "Leave me be."

"You are correct. I should change the way I address you."

Siobhan looked back at him, her eyes narrowed with suspicion. "Over the last week, I realized to not know you at all and especially that our marriage is a mistake. However there is little to be done about it, so we should set some ground rules."

As he'd suspected, Siobhan did not feel as strongly as he did. That he'd been struck ill for the past week made things worse. Of course he would agree to anything she proposed, he owed her as much, especially at having to marry a man she didn't care for.

Strange that his entire life, he'd fought against being entrapped into marriage by women who overtly admired him. And when he finally married, his bride was immune to him.

He walked to the side of the bed and pulled the cord. They waited silently until Leena appeared. "My lord?"

"Bring tea, perhaps tarts. Her ladyship and I are not to be disturbed otherwise."

Siobhan stood by the window in silence, staring out onto the grounds as he spoke to the maid.

"Would you please sit down?" Miles asked, trying his best to keep from sounding annoyed. It wasn't that he was mad at Siobhan, but he was upset about their situation and especially the lack of time he'd had to explain things, and to allow her to get to know him more.

The maid returned with the tea and poured for the silent couple. She gave him an unsure smile and left, silently closing the door behind her as she left.

Siobhan lowered into a chair but did not touch the teacup. Behind her angered expression was a flicker of hurt. He fought not to reach out to touch her.

"I apologize for being absent the past week. I should have explained certain things to you before we married. I did not make the time, because it is hard to admit."

Refusing to look at him, Siobhan instead reached for her cup and took a sip.

Miles continued, "I am afraid you have married a man who is... not fully well."

At this, she turned to him, sky blue eyes searching his face. "What do you mean?"

Having to fight past the dryness in his throat, he cleared it. "I suffer from debilitating headaches. There is nothing any doctor has been able to do to keep them at bay. They last for days on end."

"Is that why you sometimes sleep on the floor?" she blurted, her eyes widening at her disclosure. "The day we formulated the engagement, I slipped up here to find you. You seemed incoherent. I thought you to be drunk."

He let out a breath, embarrassment coating him like slimy pond water. "I suppose it would seem that way. During these times, I cannot find a place to be comfortable. Whether the bed, the floor, it matters not. The pain is without pity on me."

Her expression softened, but there remained steel in her eyes. "You should have informed me. Someone should have told me why you were in your room all those days. It was not fair."

"I agree. I am so very sorry." Miles reached for her hand, but she moved it away.

"What now?" she asked. "Am I to stay away whenever these episodes occur? And I need to know, what causes them? Do you know? Are they frequent?"

That she asked so matter-of-factly was another blow to his ego. He'd expected more compassion, or perhaps to have to assure her that he was well otherwise. Instead, she'd seemed more worried about her role.

"You should probably avoid being near me," he admitted. "I am sometimes out of my mind with pain." He looked away. "What you witnessed was not the norm, as it only lasted one day and night. It has been almost six months since the last long episode before this one. But more often than not, they last up to a week or so."

"This marriage," Siobhan began. "I do not know what to think. We have not made any decisions. It feels as if I do not have a place, a role."

"What do you wish? If you wish for our own home, I will purchase one. If you wish for us to travel, to go for more outings, balls... Just say it."

Her lips curved at him mentioning balls as they both were not at all socially inclined. "What I wish is to know you better, and it seems to me that we should live elsewhere, by ourselves."

Miles understood. Although he loved his family and the beautiful estate, he much preferred his time at the townhouse.

"Would you like to purchase a home?"

"No." Siobhan shook her head. "I like the townhouse."

"What about the other..."

She leaned forward in her chair, her blue eyes darkening. "That you have these headaches does not make you less of a man.

It is out of your control. I would like to be present when your doctor visits next. To discuss how to care for you."

Miles was struck silent. He closed his eyes and let out a long breath. "You do not have to care for me. I usually have forewarnings and can return here."

"I am your wife; it should fall upon me. I wish to do it." Siobhan stated, shaking her head. "I do not want you to have to leave our home when you do not feel well."

After a moment, when he reached for her hand, she allowed it. Their gazes clashed, neither seeming to be able to look away. In the darkened blue pools, he could see she fought not to cry.

"This morning," Miles began. "I should not have acted like I did. Upon hearing you were back there where you were abducted, all I could think of was you being hurt again."

She blinked, and an errant tear slid down her cheek. "I have to do it. It is very important to me."

"Can we wait? Let me find out more about what occurred and see what the authorities are doing about finding the man who attacked you."

Siobhan nodded. "How long?"

"Just a week, perhaps two, but no more. I promise."

CHAPTER FOURTEEN

A T DINNER, THE duchess and Penelope excitedly shared information about the upcoming fundraiser. Siobhan listened intently before finally having to ask, "What are the proceeds used for?"

Penelope shrugged good-naturedly. "For the poor."

"Where, specifically?" Siobhan asked, interested to know if perhaps some of the money could be distributed to the shelter.

The duchess replied to her question, "We have a list of places to give the funds, or provisions needed. There is a hospital for expectant mothers, a pair of orphanages, and several other charities where our funds pay for clothing, food and any repairs needed to the buildings."

"I am sure they appreciate the help. I work and help at a shelter, near St. Sebastian," she informed them. "There is a lot of need there. My friend Henriette and I also see about a sick widow named Susan. She has a trio of wee bairns and can barely get out of bed."

The duchess gave Miles a stricken look before turning back to Siobhan. "You go there personally? What exactly do you do?"

"Whatever is needed. Usually Henriette and I bring food, cook a meal, bathe the children. There is a woman who we pay to clean the small apartment."

"Now that you are titled, those tasks should be left to someone else. I am sure a pair of maids can be sent weekly." The duchess began eating, expecting Siobhan would accept the decree.

If not for Miles giving her a warning look, she would have informed his mother she was to continue to do as before. Instead, she ate as Miles began a new conversation informing the family they were to go to live at the townhouse the following morning.

After the men drank their brandy in the sitting room, and the ladies read for a bit, Siobhan stood. "I am getting sleepy. Good night, everyone."

Miles stood with her and bid everyone a good night as well. He walked with her up the stairs and instead of heading toward his bed chamber, he walked toward hers. Siobhan wasn't sure what to say, so she waited for him to bid her good night at the door.

His heavily lashed eyes met hers. "Can I stay with you tonight?"

Something in her moved, her stomach tightened, and her pulse sped up. "Yes, of course."

A part of her was glad that he wished to be with her, but another wondered who the real Miles was. The one who'd callously thrown her from his bedchamber, the angry man who'd dragged her away that morning, or this calmer, reasonable one. Perhaps he was all three.

They walked into the bedchamber, and she wondered if he'd want to join with her again. Although it wasn't altogether unpleasant, and admittedly very intimate, she was nervous that it would hurt again.

Leena entered and helped her to undress, slipping a pale pink nightgown over her head. The silky fabric caressed her skin as Siobhan slid between the covers.

After sending his valet away, Miles came to the bed bereft of clothing and lay on his side facing her. "What are you thinking?"

"That you and I do need to be alone, to spend time like this together, I believe it is important for a married couple to sleep in the same bed."

"Do your parents?" he asked.

Siobhan nodded. "Yes. Yours do not."

"At times they did, but in the last years, Father has become restless at night and moved into another bedroom to keep from bothering my mother."

When he pulled her against him, his lips seeking hers, Siobhan gave into the kiss, needing to feel a connection with Miles. Their lips lingered, discovering, until his tongue prodded past hers and into her mouth. The sensation was wonderful, she was delighted at how easily her body came to life when with him.

Somehow, he managed to reach under her nightgown, pulling the silken fabric up and up until managing to pull it off. "I wanted to tell Leena not to bother," he murmured with a playful smirk, "but I did not wish to discomfit you."

As he spoke his hands traveled over her body, sliding down her back to touch her in places that had never once been touched by any man. Every inch responded with vibrancy until she was almost breathless from it.

How was it possible for a mere touch to affect one so much? Siobhan's eyes rolled back when his mouth took the tip of her breast, while his fingers circled around her upper thigh area.

"Oh," she called out, not sure how else to respond. When his finger slid down the center of her sex, she gasped. Her being came to life, eagerly anticipating more.

Miles seemed to know exactly what to do as he splayed her open with his hand while one of his fingers caressed the very core of her.

Siobhan clutched his shoulders and pushed her head back into the pillows as the stimulation continued making heat travel outward from where he continued the delicious assault. Then to her utter delight, she shattered. Trembling in response, she cried out, lost as wave after wave of ecstasy washed over her.

Once again his mouth sought hers, this time with pure hunger; it was as if he wished to devour her entirely, and Siobhan would not have minded one bit.

Her body pulsed and she was glad when he began to enter

her, pushing his hard staff in slowly. Emboldened, she reached for the orbs of his bottom and palmed them as he thrust in fully. There was no pain; instead the ebbing sensations she'd just experienced seemed to linger.

When he began moving, his hips lifting and lowering, Siobhan could hardly understand what occurred. But she urged him to move faster, deeper to take her fully and without restraint.

Seeming to melt together, she became unaware of where he ended, and she began. All she knew was that it should never end and at the same time that she was on the verge of another climatic moment.

"Come with me," Miles whispered in her ear. "Let go."

Siobhan threw her head back and lifted her hips to meet his thrusts, once, twice, and then a bolt of release hit so hard, she splintered into a hundred pieces.

In the recess of her mind, she heard Miles' deep groan as he too climaxed, his beautiful body trembling in release.

Falling over her, she accepted the weight. It was like a balm after the storm, leaving them both breathless and sleek from the exertion.

"I missed you," Miles whispered, kissing her temple. "I really did."

Tears sprung to her eyes, and she was sure it was because of having just experienced such a wonderful moment. "I missed you as well."

SIOBHAN ARRANGED FLOWERS in a vase, deep in thought as to how to approach Miles that evening about returning to her work at the shelter. Two weeks had passed and as far as she knew, the constable had yet to capture her assailant.

A soft breeze blew in through the open window and sunlight brightened the parlor at the townhouse. Since moving there, they'd become closer, spending the evenings when he returned from working with his father, eating, taking walks and even attending a musicale.

Every evening Siobhan was giddy to experience intimacy with her husband. This night, however, it wasn't to be as her monthly courses had arrived. She sighed and turned at the sound of voices.

Jones appeared at the doorway. "You have visitors, my lady. Your mother and sister."

"Show them in please." Siobhan walked behind the butler to greet them.

Her mother scanned the room upon entering, seeming to find fault by the dourness of her expression. "Honestly, Siobhan, you should insist on living at the estate. I admit the townhouse is adequate, but you are titled now."

Used to her mother's way, the comments didn't bother her. In her opinion, if her mother was complaining about something, it meant she was in good spirits.

"This house is more than adequate for us at the moment."

Amelia shrugged as if she'd been asked her opinion. "If I would have married Miles, I would be living at the estate."

"Tea?" Siobhan asked when Firtha brought a tray of tea and cakes. She poured and waited to find out the nature of the visit. "Have you been out shopping?"

Her mother nodded. "Yes, and we came to tell you the good news." Her face brightened making Siobhan smile in return.

"What is it?"

"Your sister is engaged."

Amelia held out her hand to show off a rather large bauble. "It was his great-grandmother's, who was an honorable lady."

"Oh," Siobhan said studying the piece. "It is rather large. Probably very costly."

"We should not speak of it," her mother said and then grinned. "I am told it is worth a prince's ransom."

Amelia giggled. "Charles and I will be married at St. Paul's."

"St. Paul's?" Siobhan stated, confused that her parents would wish the ceremony to be at any place other than their own church. "Why?"

"Because it is grand and huge. That is where Eileen McIntire married, and everyone was so taken by the grandeur," Amelia said of one of her friends. "His father helped it happen."

Their mother looked on with pride. "I am so very glad about the matches you've made. Now I can rest in the knowledge that both of you married well. Hopefully soon you will provide Miles with an heir." She gave Siobhan a pointed look.

"I do wish for children," Siobhan replied. "However, I want more time with Miles, just the two of us."

"What on earth for?" her mother asked, seeming confused. "You and he will always be together. There is no need to prolong the coming of children."

Siobhan leaned forward, her sister and mother reflecting the movement. "It is because I have fallen in love with him," she said in a low tone. "I want him all to myself, at least for a little while."

Her mother rolled her eyes. "It is good when a wife comes to care for her husband. However, there is an order to things. Emotions do not come into play."

"I disagree," Miles said, walking in. His eyes locked with hers.

Siobhan hoped he'd not heard her declaration, as she wasn't sure he felt the same. If there was a time for the ground to open and her to fall in, this was it.

She lifted her hot face when he neared, and he kissed her temple. Then he went to her mother first and then her sister and kissed their cheeks. "Ladies, what a pleasant surprise."

"Amelia and Charles are engaged," Siobhan informed him as he took a seat beside her. "Am I to assume there will be a celebration?"

As her mother and sister began regaling with the plans for a grand gala, Miles kept stealing glances at her. Siobhan was convinced he'd heard her, and she was not sure how to respond to him. Although she wished with all her heart that he would come to love her, she also understood that oftentimes the best one could hope for was deep caring.

She searched his face for an inkling of what he was thinking. However, Miles was a master of masking his thoughts.

By the time her family left, they were rushed for time. Both remained in the same clothes in which they were dressed as they went to the McLeod estate to meet with Miles' friends and their wives. It would be the second time they gathered, and it seemed to Siobhan the group gathered regularly when possible for a meal.

"How often did you and your friends meet before all getting married?" Siobhan asked, liking that he held her hand.

His lips curved. "Quite often, perhaps twice, and even three times a week. We had little else to do. In fact, I didn't meet with them as often as the others. Now that they have wives, some occupations, every other week or so is the most we can muster."

"It is gratifying that the group is making an effort not to grow apart." Siobhan looked on as Miles lifted her hand to his lips. "I feel the same." His heated gaze met hers. "I cannot wait to return home and have you all to myself."

A sigh escaped her. "There can be no intimacy for at least four days," she informed him with a frown.

"Oh," he replied, "I see." He recovered and kissed her hand again. "I am content to share the bed with my beautiful wife."

Siobhan chuckled.

The evening was enjoyable. Siobhan mentioned to them wishing she could invite Henriette and her brother to join them during their gatherings knowing the group would adore her friends. Felicity lifted both hands in excitement. "Of course. It would be exciting to have French guests. Please ask them to join us next week."

When the women asked how she knew them, Miles turned from his conversation with Henry and Grant to listen. Siobhan was sure he waited to hear what she'd say about the shelter and Susan. But it did not stop her from telling the other three women about what she and Henriette did most Saturdays.

"How honorable," Hannah, Henry's wife, exclaimed. "I would love to join you one day."

"I would as well," Wren, who'd recently married Felicity's brother Grant, added.

The last woman, Felicity, shook her head. "I suppose that means I shall join as well. I can't imagine remaining home while the lot of you save the world."

"I do not think it is safe," Miles interrupted. "Siobhan was attacked there, and the culprit has yet to be caught."

Henry nodded in agreement. "The lot of you will stand out. You may as well be holding signs asking to be robbed."

"I believe that by bringing along a few men, we will be very safe," Wren eyed Grant. "Would you not accompany me?"

Grant, who was the most recently married of Miles' friends, looked at the other men, seeming at a loss as to which side to take. "You know I will," he finally admitted.

Felicity let out a bark of laughter. "A gaggle of posh people descending will set all kinds of things into motion. I prefer our husbands stay away. We can wear serviceable gowns and…"

"Why don't you plan something separate?" Evan asked. "Perhaps once a month, we can set up and give things away to the needy."

Siobhan had to admit it was a good idea, but she considered Susan and her brood. She didn't want to abandon them.

The women began to discuss the possibilities, becoming enthusiastic about the prospect of planning for their new venture. Her admiration grew for her new friends at their excitement to help those less fortunate.

CHAPTER FIFTEEN

A year later…

MILES RETURNED AFTER spending the morning meeting with Grant, Evan and Henry at the Grant Hotel, discussing the near return of the ship in which they'd invested. A missive had arrived that the ship was due back any day.

They would all become very rich men, once the precious cargo arrived. Already every bit of it was sold and all that needed to happen was for it to arrive safely.

Although already wealthy in his own right, Miles was glad to have secured even more of a stable future for his wife and future family.

He looked up at the townhouse, shaking his head as he recalled Siobhan's reluctance to move to a larger home. Even now as he considered approaching her once again about the subject, he wondered what her response would be.

Upon entering, he had to admit the townhouse was nothing like it had been before marrying. The drapery was now a pale gray, and there were bright flowers visible through the windows in what had been a small garden with only shrubbery. His once very bachelor bedroom drenched in dark greens and browns had been redecorated, the walls papered in flower patterns, the bedding in shades of rose, and thankfully for his masculine senses, a soft gray.

He noted that Siobhan was absent from the parlor, so Miles asked Jones, "Is my wife napping?"

"No sir, she stated that she had plans outside the house, to-day. Firtha tried to dissuade her, but she and Leena left right after you."

Immediately he realized it was Saturday, and his heart sank. "Where did she say she would be going?"

Just as Jones was about to answer, the door opened, and a bright-faced Siobhan walked in. Both she and Leena's arms spilled over with bundles. She bustled into the parlor, smiling brightly.

"Oh pooh, I'd hoped to beat you home." She allowed his kiss, blushing prettily. "I spent most of the morning with Wren and the new wee bairn. You should see him, Miles. He is so beautiful."

Since Wren had delivered, just a week prior, Siobhan had found every excuse to visit. She'd fallen in love immediately with Grant's son, a healthy boy named Byron.

"First I lose you to Henry's little girl and now to another wee one," he teased. "How are mother and son faring?"

It was heartwarming to see how easily Siobhan had warmed to children now that all his friends were fathers. Henry and Hannah had been blessed with a beautiful baby girl they'd called Helena, Evan and Felicity were expecting their second child, the first being a boy.

When Siobhan straightened, her hands went to the small of her back and she pressed into it with a groan. As she arched, the round mound of her swollen midsection became evident.

Approaching the subject with care, he smiled indulgently at his beautiful wife. "The doctor advised that you should not be out and about so much this far into your pregnancy."

Siobhan frowned. "I am young and strong. It makes little sense to sit about all day. I am not ill, Miles. I am expecting a child, a most natural thing."

Pushing away from him, she sat down and motioned for him to join her on the settee. "You must see the beautiful things I've purchased for our wee one."

It was a long while before every item was displayed for his

perusal. By the end, he'd begun praying for there not to be more than one item in each bundle.

After his wife and Leena left the parlor to take the items to the nursery, he stood to pour a glass of brandy.

Despite both their mothers asking that they live at one of the larger estates to await the arrival of the bairn, a very stubborn Siobhan had insisted she'd rather have their child at home. He'd been charged by his mother to approach the subject again.

"Miles," Siobhan appeared in the doorway. "I believe there are items missing from the nursery."

"I am sure there are not. Perhaps Firtha rearranged them. You should ask her."

She narrowed her eyes. "Have your mother or mine been here?"

It was the best time to tell her. "Yes, both Mother and Penelope were here. I am sure they enjoyed seeing the nursery."

"Why would they come when I wasn't here?" Siobhan walked into the parlor and paced. "Are they up to something?"

Just as he was about to tell her they were moving to the Johnstone estate until after the birth, Jones appeared.

"My Lord, a constable is here."

"Stay here." He hurried to the door, where a man in uniform stood. Behind him two others held a familiar man who struggled to get free.

The constable introduced himself, his eyes moving from Miles to behind him, where he knew Siobhan hovered in spite of his orders to remain where she was. Spirited woman, his wife, driving him mad with desire at times and just plain mad at others. He rolled his eyes to himself, and bit back a grin.

"Is this the man who accosted your wife, my lord?" the serious man asked.

He studied the man to make sure; the last thing he wished was to accuse an innocent man of something so heinous as attempted kidnapping and who knew what else. But there was no doubt.

"It is."

Siobhan's peered out from beside him, despite his attempt to hold her back. "Is that him?" she asked, her wide eyes taking in the now-cursing man.

"Siobhan, I do not wish for you to become distressed." He took her gently by the arms. "Go back inside."

Leaning sideways, she glared at the prisoner. "You are a horrible person!" she yelled.

Again, Miles had to keep from smiling at her antics. He turned to the constable. "Thank you for continuing your search. The streets are safer for it."

"Of course, my lord," the constable replied, sticking out his chest at the compliment.

"One moment. Wait here, please." Miles went inside and retrieved a sum of notes which he handed to the constable. "One third each for bringing him to justice."

The constable's eyes widened at the amount. "Thank you, my lord. Thank you." He went to the other two, showing them the money, and both bobbed their heads, calling out their appreciation.

He continued watching as the now-docile man was put into the back of the constable's wagon to be taken to jail and as it rolled down the street.

Now that the worry of the man perhaps planning to come again for Siobhan was gone, he had to deal with a larger foe: getting his spitfire of a wife to agree to go to the estate for a few months.

THE HEALTHY CRIES filled the corridor and Miles burst into the bedchamber, much to the annoyance of the mid-wife and the other women present.

Siobhan lay in the middle of the bed, dark locks plastered to her wet face, her face red from the delivery. With her eyes closed, she looked to be too exhausted to do more than breathe.

He rushed to her side. "Is something wrong?" He searched the other women's faces, but they all seemed unable to find the correct reply. "Tell me."

"Will you be quiet for a moment," Siobhan snapped suddenly, in a surprisingly strong voice. "I am trying to revel in the lack of pain. I am told another round will begin in a moment."

He took her hand, and she snatched it away. "Give me my bairn," she demanded.

Overcome with worry for Siobhan, Miles had momentarily forgotten about the babe and now he watched as the midwife wrapped the small, squalling infant and turned to hand the bundle to Miles' mother.

"A boy," his mother annoyed, tears streaming down her face. "I finally have a grandchild."

"The child will not have a grandmother if you do not give him to me," Siobhan said with a chuckle.

The babe was lowered and quickly nestled into Siobhan's arms. "What a beauty you are," she said, taking in the infant. "What a beautiful boy you are."

With downy dark hair and rosy cheeks, Miles wondered who he'd look like most. The true color of the babe's eyes would not be evident for a while yet.

"We shall call him Leon Owen Johnstone," Siobhan announced. "After his grandfathers."

His mother sniffed. "They will be so very pleased."

Later when they were finally left alone, Miles looked on as the newborn latched onto Siobhan's engorged breast, drinking greedily. He would be healthy and robust by the way the boy partook of the offering.

"How do you feel?" he asked, pressing a kiss to his wife's temple.

"I am tired, if I may be honest. Once he finishes, I wish to sleep for a week."

Miles smiled. "From what I hear, the staff is having difficulty keeping our friends at bay. You will have to wait a bit to rest."

Her laughter was like a balm to his soul.

If asked just a year ago, never would Miles have thought a moment with a wife and child, would be the happiest of his life.

THE END

ABOUT THE AUTHOR

Most days USA Today Bestseller Hildie McQueen can be found in her overly tight leggings and green hoodie, holding a cup of British black tea while stalking her hunky lawn guy. Author of Medieval Highlander and American Historical romance, she writes something every reader can enjoy.

Hildie's favorite past-times are reader conventions, traveling, shopping and reading.

She resides in beautiful small town Georgia with her super-hero husband Kurt and three little doggies.

Visit her website at www.hildiemcqueen.com
Facebook: HildieMcQueen
Twitter: @HildieMcQueen
Instagram: hildiemcqueenwriter

9 781963 585377